GHOST CAT

Look for these and
other Apple Paperbacks
in your local bookstore!

The Dollhouse Murders
by Betty Ren Wright

Christina's Ghost
by Betty Ren Wright

Secrets in the Attic
by Carol Beach York

The Haunting
by Margaret Mahy

Haunted Island
by Joan Lowery Nixon

Jamie and the Mystery Quilt
by Vicki Berger Erwin

GHOST CAT

Beverly Butler

AN
APPLE
PAPERBACK

SCHOLASTIC INC.
New York Toronto London Auckland Sydney

My special thanks to Dr. Otto Keller and
Melva Keller for their advice on the clinical
aspects and treatment of asthma.

ISBN 0-590-43443-8

12 11 10 9 8   3 4/9

For Liz and Matt

1

A cat was crying somewhere.

The sound dragged Annabel up through layers of sleep. Muffin! The alarm shredded the last tatters of her dreams. Muffin's got herself shut outdoors somehow and can't get in.

Annabel was sitting up on the edge of the bed, fumbling for her slippers with her toes before she got her eyes really open. She blinked at the big, attic bedroom sparsely furnished with two heavy, old-fashioned chests of drawers, a vanity table and mirror, and two wide brass beds just growing visible in the half light of early morning. Where were her bookcases? Her record player? And the big, over-stuffed platform rocker that left her barely space to turn around in her cramped little room but that was so cozy to curl up in?

Recollection came like the rip of adhesive tape off raw skin. Her own snug room in Chicago was hundreds of miles away. She was stuck in a hundred-year-old farmhouse in the Northwoods of Wisconsin, sentenced to spend the summer on a defunct farm among relatives she didn't know, so that her mother could be free to indulge in an array of wonderful new interests that left her no time to waste in the company of a gawky, teenage daughter.

The cat outside cried again, ripped the final inch of adhesive away. For it wasn't Muffin. It couldn't be.

Annabel herself, three weeks ago, had gathered Muffin's crushed gold-and-white body up from the pavement where it lay stiffened near the skid marks of tires that had swerved in vain to avoid killing—or deliberately to accomplish it. Muffin, whose love for Annabel had been as real and uncomplicated as Annabel's for her.

The familiar sting of tears began to smart inside Annabel's eyelids. She was tempted to press her face into the pillow and weep her grief into the muffling folds as she had done so often before, but the cat, the other cat, was still crying. It wasn't Muffin, but it was a cat in distress. The mewing was plaintive, questing, and manifestly unhappy. Annabel couldn't simply roll back into bed and ignore it.

Moving quietly so as not to disturb her cousin Donna asleep in the next bed, she jammed her long legs into a pair of jeans, stuffed her feet into socks and sneakers, and pulled a baggy T-shirt down over her head.

She and Donna had been acquainted now for two days, and they had yet to find anything they shared in common beyond a great-grandfather long-since dead and the fact that they were both fourteen. It went without saying that

8

Donna was the pretty one: trim, graceful and dainty and a good eight inches less than Annabel's gangly five-foot-eleven and three-quarters.

Predictably, Annabel's elbow knocked a hairbrush off the top of the chest as she tried to tiptoe by. By luck it landed softly on the braided rug below, and Donna didn't wake up.

Annabel managed to negotiate the steep, uncarpeted stairs without more than a few creaks to mark her descent. The deep hush of a house still asleep breathed in the air.

She paused at the foot of the attic stairs to glance along the bedroom hall. The first door was Aunt Lil's and Uncle Axel's—her father's aunt and uncle, actually, and the grandparents of Donna and the other cousins. Across from it was Michael's, Donna's twelve-year-old brother. Next to that was Todd's, a cousin who had arrived late yesterday evening. He was a puffy, pallid boy of fifteen who, according to Donna, suffered asthma attacks when he was upset, and so had to have a room to himself.

Todd had been coming here every summer for years to escape the ozone alerts that hot weather brought to Milwaukee, where he lived. Donna and Michael, who hailed from Minneapolis, had spent part of the last three summers here. Annabel alone had never set foot on the family farm before.

"Which is all the more reason to get busy and make yourself at home," Aunt Lil had declared, her round, un-wrinkled face one welcoming smile in its frame of silver-gray hair. Aunt Lil promised to be the summer's one saving grace. "I've always been sorry we never had the chance to know your father better. The more family I can round up in one place, the happier I am."

The three bedroom doors were firmly closed without a whisper of movement behind any of them to suggest anyone was awake. How was it that no one but Annabel seemed to hear the forlorn mewing outside? Or was it that an animal in distress didn't matter that much to anyone but her?

To her, the continuing sound was becoming a force she couldn't resist if she tried. She tiptoed on down the next flight of stairs and across the living room to the front door. The door swung open at her touch as if it had been waiting. Weird, she reflected, to be living so far off the beaten track that people didn't trouble to lock their doors at night.

On the wide front porch that ran the length of the house she halted to listen. For the moment there was silence everywhere. A misting rain was falling noiselessly. Not a leaf rustled nor a bird chirped, although the pale light was growing stronger.

Then, there it was: that anguished mew. It came from the direction of the barn. No, from the woods behind the barn.

Annabel set out at a loping run through the wet grass. She thought of traps that might be in the woods, rabbit snares or steel-jawed things, and immediately tried not to. It was sad enough that the poor creature was bewildered and lost and getting rained on into the bargain.

"Here, kitty. Here, kitty, kitty," she called as she neared the barn.

A deep growl greeted her from inside the barn. A massive black shadow rose up in the doorway.

Annabel slowed to a wary walk. "Ricky? Good boy. Nice dog. It's just me."

He was a difficult dog to get to know, a mixture of several breeds, none of them small and all of them nervous. She had made a certain amount of headway toward becoming friends in the past two days, but there was no predicting when a hand extended to him would be met by a lopsided wag of his great corkscrew of a tail or by a warning show of teeth.

"Nice Ricky," she said, coming to a prudent standstill beside the door. "You remember me. It's okay. It's all right."

He wasn't looking at her, nor listening to her either. His head was turned to the woods. Another growl rumbled up from his huge chest as the cat mewed again. The hair along his spine rose in a bristling ridge.

"Ricky, no!" Annabel said sharply, alarmed now for the cat's safety. Suppose the dog should rush ahead of her and seize the cat in those fierce jaws before she could get to it? "Back! Stay back."

The dog swung his head around with a half-whimper, half-growl as if he had only just now discovered she was there. He was trembling as though he had been beaten.

Annabel put out a careful hand and stroked his head lightly. He whined uneasily and slid away from her, cringing into the shadows inside the barn. It was quite apparent that he had no desire to join her on her cat hunt.

Nevertheless, Annabel took a long step forward and closed the bottom half of the divided door, shutting him in to be absolutely sure. "Weird," she told herself for the second time that morning.

She sprinted the last dozen yards to the edge of the woods. The cat was still repeating its mournful cries but they were growing fainter, receding farther into the trees. Ricky's growling had probably scared it into retreat.

Well, that was proof she needn't worry anymore about a trap.

"Here, kitty, kitty," she called. "Come, kitty. Come."

The mewing stopped short. Was the cat listening?

"Kitty," Annabel repeated. "Kitty, kitty, kitty."

Utter silence.

She crouched down on her heels, trying to peer through the hip-high tangle of brambles and fern that blotted out any trace of a path into the woods if there had ever been one.

"Kitty, kitty," she called twice more, and waited.

The absolute quiet under the trees was almost creepy. It felt as if the whole place were holding its breath and watching. Watching her. She rubbed her hand over the little prickles of gooseflesh that were popping up on her arm beneath the flecks of rain.

"Kitty?" she tried again.

The answering meow was so close she jumped.

"Kitty!" She made her voice soft with sympathy and persuasion. "Come, kitty. Come on."

Another meow. Then, there he was. For the briefest of instants she saw him gazing at her from under the dripping fronds of a fern: a big gray-and-white cat with long, silken fur that looked as soft as thistledown.

Suddenly, without a flicker of motion he was gone. Dissolved into nothing but a tracery of dark ferns against the pale trunk of a huge, old birch.

"Kitty," Annabel coaxed. "Come, kitty. Come, puss. Come—" The name slipped into her mind unbidden but somehow right—"Duff, Macduff."

He answered her, but from a little farther off and to her left. She called again, and again he answered, but from an even greater distance.

For a while she went on calling, listening to his replies, always prompt and eager, growing ever more remote. When she gave up, baffled, the same thick, eerie silence settled down on the woods as before.

A shiver crawled the length of her spine under her damp T-shirt, although she wasn't really cold. This was a spooky place, this stretch of woods with its crowding of rigid black trunks lightened only here and there by a ghostly birch, all of them still only half-solid forms in the morning mist. She could imagine the cat a victim of some ancient curse by which any creature that ventured into these woods was doomed to roam in a hopeless circle forever, never able to break free.

"Kitty!" she called once more, loudly, to shake off such morbid fancies.

She stood up to ease the cramps in her legs. The cat mewed abruptly from almost as nearby as when she had seen it, except that it was approaching from her right this time.

She thrust aside the thought that the animal actually did seem to be traveling in a circle. A better explanation was that, much as the cat wanted to be rescued, it had been chased by dogs and heartless humans so often that it was afraid to show itself in the open. Her coaxing might be more effective if she ventured partway into the woods herself.

She glanced up and down the edges of the woods in search of a break in the heavy underbrush that would be easier to push through. There was none. She was gripped suddenly by an odd reluctance to set foot past the closest tree, let alone wade on into the mysterious dimness beyond.

The cat mewed plaintively.

"Now I'm getting weird," Annabel told her foolish qualms.

She hitched up her jeans and resolutely strode straight forward into the ferns. At once she was drenched to the skin from thigh to ankle by a deluge of water from the fronds. A raspberry bramble whipped across the back of one knee and imbedded its thorns in the fabric covering the other. She had to stop.

"Wait, kitty. I'll be there," she called as she stooped to drag off the stubborn briars.

"Let it be, girl," said a reedy voice behind her.

Annabel's gasp tore her free and whirled her around. She was hardly less startled to see that the speaker was the old man whose bedroom opened off the living room. Old Pa was what everyone called him. He was Aunt Lil's father and, according to Donna, well into his nineties. Annabel had seen him only at mealtimes, when he shuffled from his room to the table and sat picking at his food without a comment to anyone.

"What did you say?"

The old man blinked at her through rain-speckled glasses. "I say let it be."

"What? The cat?" Or did he mean she shouldn't be crashing through raspberries that would probably be producing a fine harvest of berries later on? "There's a lost cat in there. It's crying. I've got to help it."

She rustled clear of the bushes and sidestepped farther to her right. The cat wasn't crying now. The sound of Old Pa's voice had stopped it. "Kitty?" she called.

"I say leave it, girl!"

The sharp authority in the command rather than the command itself halted her.

"Why?" Annabel demanded. Then accusingly, "You've scared it away."

The old man's head began to shake either from palsy or disapproval. He hunched bent shoulders inside his faded yellow sweater. "That one don't scare. And you don't want him. If he's out, she'll be stirring soon."

"Who will? Aunt Lil?" Annabel asked even as the suspi-

15

cion was growing in her that it might be unrealistic to expect him to make sense. "Aunt Lil doesn't have a cat."

Aside from Ricky, this place boasted no livestock of any kind. Annabel had looked forward to making the acquaintance of a variety of animals here as at least some compensation for her exile from home. She got on a lot better with animals, generally, than she did with people.

But although the property had been known as the Peterson farm from the time one of her Peterson ancestors had homesteaded it more than a century ago, it hadn't been an active, working farm for a good many years. Uncle Axel Peterson, an executive in the paper mill in town until his retirement, limited his farming efforts to a large vegetable garden behind the kitchen and to the maintenance of a well-trimmed lawn.

"She'll be stirring soon," Old Pa repeated, his voice reedy and cracked once more. He seemed to be addressing the crook of the cane he clasped in both thin hands. "Always when there's young folks by. That's when she don't rest easy."

Annabel shifted from one foot to the other. She wanted to find the cat. It would be wandering off discouraged if she didn't keep up her coaxing and calling.

Yet, would it be right to leave the old man by himself, at sea in a mental fog?

A door banged up at the house. Aunt Lil's voice fluted across the yard. "Pa? Pa, where are you? Are you outside?"

Old Pa turned his back on the direction of the voice. He jabbed his cane to this side and that of a red clover as if he hadn't heard. It was possible, Annabel supposed, that he hadn't.

"Over here," she called. "By the woods. He's with me."

She waved as Aunt Lil's round form in corduroy slacks and print apron trotted into view beyond the barn.

Aunt Lil halted. "Pa, for heaven's sake! What are you doing clear off there and in all this wet? You'll be crippled up for a month. Bring him back to the house, Annabel, will you, please?"

"There's a lost cat in there." Annabel swept her arm to indicate the trees. "I'm trying to find it."

"That's all right. Don't worry about it," Aunt Lil said in the cheery tone of one who wasn't really listening. "You come in, too, and change into something dry. I've got breakfast started."

Old Pa was scowling at the clover and shaking his head. "Bad business," he muttered beneath his breath. "Shouldn't be here. Shouldn't have to be here."

Whether he was referring to himself, the clover, Aunt Lil, or something totally different, Annabel couldn't guess.

He might as well be talking about her. She shouldn't be here. Shouldn't have to be here.

She wouldn't be, either, except for Donald—Dr. Donald Kimball, with his white teeth and cleft chin and Burt Reynolds mustache. They would like her to believe, he and her mother, that she was here because this was the ideal time for her to get acquainted with her father's side of the family. Or that she was too solitary and would benefit from a summer in the company of cousins her own age.

Or that she would be at loose ends and too much on her own at home with her mother taking special evening courses at the university and working at the clinic all day.

Annabel wasn't buying any of that. For as far back as she could remember, the annual Christmas card from the farm had carried in it an invitation to come up and visit. Always, especially in the five years since the death of her father, Uncle Axel's nephew, it was dismissed as too remote a possibility even to warrant discussion. There was plenty in Chicago to keep her occupied—her books, her bike, swimming lessons, TV. And how often had her mother said she didn't know how she would have managed these last years without Annabel's company.

They had managed, just the two of them together. They hadn't asked for help from anyone else. They hadn't needed anyone but each other.

That was until this past Easter. Then Dr. Donald Kimball—not even a real doctor but a dentist—had joined the clinic. He also joined the clinic car pool, and very soon was dropping Mom off last when it was his turn to drive.

And he was leaving magazines on natural history for Annabel, bringing a catnip mouse for Muffin (which Muffin, clever creature that she was, promptly batted under the sofa and never touched again), providing theater tickets and dinner for three on Mom's birthday, suggesting that Mom look into refresher courses in her field as lab technician, and encouraging her to broaden her interests outside of work.

Mom kept insisting he was no more than a considerate

friend, but all at once the burning question had become how to dispose of Annabel for the summer. Annabel was in the way.

Her scowl matched that of Old Pa's as she slipped a hand under his arm. "Aunt Lil wants us to go in. She's getting breakfast."

Old Pa jerked his elbow away. "I brought myself out here. I guess I got sense enough to bring myself in."

Annabel retreated an apologetic step. "Sure. Okay."

She didn't know much about old folks or how they were supposed to be treated.

Thank goodness, here was Aunt Lil advancing on them.

"Come on, Pa, you're dawdling, and you're getting wetter by the minute." Aunt Lil seized his arm in a no-nonsense grip that caused him to lurch against his cane for balance.

"You heard it, didn't you? The cat?" he asked as she started him forward. "She's sent it out. It's having these youngsters about. They've got her started."

"Now don't start that kind of talk. You know how it upsets Axel." Aunt Lil actually gave his arm a small shake. "There isn't any cat. Never was in my experience. And we always have children here during the summer."

"Not children this year. Young folks," Old Pa repeated stubbornly. "You watch them close or she'll be stirring."

"It's you I'll have to be watching, if you're going to go wandering off at any hour in any weather. Really, Pa, I'm too old to be chasing after you all the time."

It was the first time that Annabel had heard her sound cross. No doubt Aunt Lil had good cause, but Annabel's

19

sympathies followed Old Pa as he was hustled across the yard. How must it be to have lived nearly a hundred years, to have grown up, worked, married, raised children, run your own life as an adult, only to end up being handled and scolded like a baby?

Annabel hung back to scan the fringes of the woods one last time. "Kitty?" she said experimentally to a clump of ferns.

There was no answer. She hadn't really expected there would be. The cat was too shy to betray itself when there were so many voices and people close-by.

With a sigh, Annabel turned her steps toward the house. She would take up the hunt later on as soon as she got the chance, maybe with a bit of food borrowed from Ricky's dish to tempt the cat into trusting her. Time enough after they were friends to worry about what to do next in this peculiar household where the very word "cat" apparently rubbed Uncle Axel wrong, and Aunt Lil, for some mysterious reason, wanted Old Pa to believe there was no such thing.

Ricky was scratching at the barn door. Annabel detoured to open it and set him free.

He paused on the threshold to sniff her hand, then her wet pants leg. His tongue flicked across her fingers, and his tail performed a lopsided wag. The raised hackles and bared teeth of half an hour ago might never have been.

"Yes, you're safe, you chicken," Annabel said, rubbing him gently between the ears. "The terrible, scary old pussy-cat is gone."

As she spoke, daylight broke through the mist, thinning the grayness to silver. The brooding blacks and charcoals of the woods brightened to tones of green and brown that were still somber because of the overcast, but no more sinister than a pretty scene on a picture postcard.

Annabel walked on, thinking of the beautiful, big fluffy cat and listening to the sodden squish of her sneakers. Only then did it cross her mind as odd that the cat's coat could have been that splendidly fluffy, not in the least bedraggled, after prowling through all that dripping foliage.

2

Annabel pulled off her soaked shoes in the linoleum-floored back entry. She padded on through the kitchen in her damp stocking feet.

"You go right on upstairs and change into something dry," Aunt Lil said, bustling into the kitchen to extract a tablespoon from a drawer. "Oh, and Annabel—" She halted midway across the big kitchen on her way back to Old Pa's room. "About Old Pa. He's a very old man, you know, and he's been sick . . ."

"Sure," Annabel said, and waited, for to judge by the troubled pucker of Aunt Lil's brows and underlip, these remarks were only the preface to something more.

But Aunt Lil abruptly gave her head a little shake. Her expression cleared, and she patted Annabel lightly on the arm. "You're a good girl," she said, and trotted off on her errand to Old Pa.

Annabel went on to the stairway, dangling her shoes from two fingers. There was no need to strive for quiet on the steps any longer. The house was now definitely awake. A radio was blaring alternate snatches of static and music from someone's bedroom. Water was running in the bathroom, and Todd was beating on a door and shrilling, "You're time's up, Donna. Get out of there."

He glared at Annabel as she reached the landing. "Everybody gets six minutes in the bathroom in the morning. And everybody takes turns. You're last in line."

He stalked on pudgy bare feet down the hall toward her as far as Michael's open door. "Hey, Michael. I told you I wanted that timer of yours. Where is it?"

A tousled Michael, one foot in a brown sock, one in an unlaced sneaker, appeared in the doorway. "Catch."

He tossed a small styrofoam box at his cousin with more thrust than aim. Todd made a grab for it and missed as it soared past his head. It struck the opposite wall about two feet above him and tumbled to rest behind the wooden spindles that topped a pendulum clock.

"Clever," Todd said. His leap to dislodge it brought only a jangle of protest from the clock chimes.

The box was well beyond his reach, which he proved by two more fruitless jumps, the second of which nearly knocked the clock off the wall.

"Here, let me." Annabel pushed him aside and, rising slightly on tiptoe, handed it down to him.

She saw her mistake at once in the swift narrowing of Todd's white-fringed eyes.

"Oh, wow! Geraldine Giraffe to the rescue." He flung his

23

head back like a man squinting up at a spire. "I bet you always eat all your palm leaves."

She had surmised yesterday when they first met that he would have found her more acceptable if she weren't a head taller than he. Now she'd added injury to insult by casually showing him up for the shorty he was—and in front of a witness.

What stung most was the snort of amusement he evoked from Michael at her expense. As if it were by her own choice that from kindergarten on she had never had to wonder where to stand when a teacher directed the class to line up according to height.

"You're cute." She flattened her hand none too gently on the limp straw that served Todd for hair. "Which one are you supposed to be? Dopey or Grumpy?"

Michael's laugh was equally responsive to her put-down of Todd.

Annabel started up the attic stairs, feeling the score was fairly even. Her stockinged foot slipped on the worn treads and she stumbled clumsily, knocking her knee painfully against the step above and causing her to lose her grip on both her shoes. Todd's derisive hoot was ringing in her ears the rest of the way up and after she gained the seclusion of the bedroom as well.

She peeled off her socks and tossed them toward the dresser. Who could blame her for preferring the company of cats and dogs to people?

Dry-shod again and in fresh jeans, she hesitated a while at the top of the stairs. Why not dawdle up here until

Aunt Lil clanged the old school bell that signaled breakfast was ready?

And let Todd think he had her on the run?

She remembered her father's advice the time he had found her crying over taunts the girls on the school bus had thought were hilarious. "Of course you're bigger than they are," he had said, his arm strong and secure around her. "There's more to you than to any two of them. What you want to do is show them that you know it."

She straightened her spine and marched on down the steps.

Her reward was to find the upstairs hall deserted. The bathroom door was still shut, music still blared from Michael's room, and Todd's door was half-open, but she saw no one and no one saw her. There was only the grim-faced man in an old-fashioned suit who scowled out at her from a huge photograph framed on the wall near the clock. The photograph was of Oscar Peterson, Uncle Axel's father and her great-grandfather. His stormy eyes had the disconcerting quality of seeming to be focused on her from no matter what angle she viewed him.

She ran on down the rest of the stairs and contrived to be in her place at the table along with Uncle Axel and Old Pa by the time Aunt Lil's bell brought the others straggling into the kitchen.

"You said I should sleep late if I wanted to," Todd accused his grandmother as he dragged his chair out from the table and plopped himself on it. "How am I supposed to sleep with everybody shouting and talking outdoors right under my window? What was going on out there? A jabber convention?"

"Nothing serious." Aunt Lil set a laden plate in front of him. "Old Pa got a little confused and wandered off outdoors, but Annabel helped me find him. Everything's all right now. No harm done."

Annabel followed the quick glance she sent toward Uncle Axel, who was helping himself from the bowl of scrambled eggs. He was a quiet, white-haired man who usually let Aunt Lil do most of the talking and confined himself to a nod or a half-smile of agreement now and then. His eyes behind the lenses of his glasses were a mild blue with pleasant crinkles at the corners, but she saw for the first time that he bore a certain resemblance to the forbidding man in the photograph, enough of a resemblance to persuade her to let Aunt Lil describe the incident this morning her own way without correction.

"Well, when I gave up and did get out of bed," Todd continued the recital of his grievances, "I couldn't get in the bathroom. She was in there. Washing her hair." He jabbed an outraged finger toward Donna.

Donna lightly touched the halo of gold fluff that framed her face. "I wash my hair every morning. If I don't, it's a disaster."

In her trim red-and-white striped turtleneck and lemon jeans, she looked about as familiar with disaster as a fashion model in *Seventeen*.

Annabel bent her head over her plate. Although passably clean, her dark hair lay on her shoulders in pretty much

26

the same haphazard jumble in which it had happened to fall when she'd rolled out of bed in such a hurry this morning. She hadn't thought to put brush or comb to it since.

Come to think of it, she was the only dark-haired person at this table and the only one whose eyes were hazel instead of some shade of blue or other. Just one more way in which she stuck out like a clay flower pot in the midst of china teacups.

She nibbled without much interest at a piece of sausage. Ordinarily she was a toast-and-orange-juice person at breakfast, but Aunt Lil didn't consider the meal worth the name unless the menu boasted meat and eggs and fried potatoes and slices of buttered toast thick with strawberry jam. Today there were waffles and syrup besides, no doubt in honor of Todd's arrival. Her stomach quailed at the prospect of being expected to do justice to so much food, but this was not the day to make an issue of how small her appetite really was.

"There's a bathroom downstairs now, too," Aunt Lil was soothing Todd. "It's new since you were here last summer. We had it put in when we were fixing over the back parlor to be Old Pa's room."

"So he could move in here and ruin everybody's beauty sleep?" Todd asked through a mouthful of waffle.

Donna and Michael giggled as if this were a delightful witticism. Even Uncle Axel chuckled faintly. Annabel grinned a little, too, to demonstrate she could be a good sport, although she wasn't altogether convinced that Todd had meant it as a joke.

She felt a trifle uncomfortable about letting Old Pa receive the full blame for a commotion in which she had had as much part as he. It couldn't matter much, though, to a person who appeared only half-aware of what was going on around him and able to comprehend less than half of that.

She shot an apologetic look at him across the table and was startled to find he was staring at her.

"Who's that girl?" he demanded suddenly and loudly of the table at large, and pointed at her.

"Why, Pa," Aunt Lil said. "You know who she is. That's Annabel. I've told you she's Axel's nephew's girl. She's from Chicago."

Uncle Axel raised his voice slightly as Old Pa continued to stare. "Annabel. Her name's Annabel Peterson."

"Sure it's not Clarabell?" Todd murmured in an aside to Michael that was meant to be overheard. "Clarabell the cow?"

Annabel drained her glass of orange juice while her cousins tittered. Todd needn't preen himself on his cleverness. There was no play on her name she hadn't heard before. He would really enjoy himself when he learned that her complete name was Annabel Lee. It had been her grandmother's name, her father had said. But to most people it was a poem about a beautiful girl so delicate she had been extinguished by a puff of wind, and they found the comparison to Annabel Peterson a choice bit of humor.

"Chicago. Axel's nephew in Chicago? That would be—"

Old Pa's mouth worked in a silent attempt to capture the memory.

"Drew," Annabel supplied. "Andrew Walter Peterson. But they called him Drew."

"Andrew Walter," Old Pa repeated, as if they were syllables strange to his ears. "Walter—" His vague expression gave way to one of recognition. He leveled a gnarled finger at Annabel. "That girl's—"

"My brother Walter's granddaughter. Yes," Uncle Axel said, snipping each word off short and sharp.

"Never mind all that, Pa," Aunt Lil put in quickly. "What matters is that her name is Annabel and she's part of the family, and we're glad to have her here."

"Maybe," Old Pa muttered, still staring at Annabel. "But maybe you won't be so glad in a while. Having that girl here, maybe you're asking for trouble."

"You bet. *Big* trouble," Todd said, setting the cousins' end of the table to giggling again.

Annabel slouched lower in her chair. She would gladly have vanished altogether.

"Annabel's all right, Pa. She's just fine." Aunt Lil was reaching for the syrup. "Here. Have you tasted your waffle yet?"

"She heard the cat," the old man's cracked voice broke through her attempt to distract him. "She was following it into the woods."

"A cat?" Michael asked, ready for another reason to giggle.

Todd tapped his temple and pointed over his head at

Old Pa, taking little care to hide the gesture from the old man.

Annabel raised her head and sat up straight. She didn't doubt that Todd was right: Old Pa's mental powers were out of business. But poking fun at a person too fuddled to defend himself struck her as being about the same as kicking a dog with a broken leg.

"Just an ordinary cat," she said. "I heard it crying like it was lost, so I went out to find it, but it ran away. A big, gray cat with white markings."

"Are you sure it wasn't a white cat with gray markings?" Todd asked, and Michael was once more convulsed.

Annabel gave them both a withering look. "It was gray with white markings: white paws and chest and a white M on its face."

Uncle Axel's cup rattled on its saucer. "That's not my idea of funny, Annabel."

Annabel blinked at him. She hadn't supposed he could speak so harshly. What was this, Pick on Annabel Day?

Todd grinned at her as he crammed a chunk of dripping waffle into his mouth. "M for mistake."

"M for Macduff," Annabel said flatly, as if the name she had happened to think of for the cat were a known fact.

"Enough!" Uncle Axel pushed his chair from the table and stood up. "I told you that's not funny, Annabel. I don't want to hear anymore about it from any of you." He glared around the circle of abashed silence he had created. His eyebrows were an angry slash of white in a face gone dull red. "And while we're on the subject, the same goes for poking into deserted buildings or anything of that sort you may have in mind, too. There's plenty of things to occupy you kids right here without meddling in matters that don't concern you."

He tramped out of the kitchen while the silence behind him was still quivering.

Annabel bit her lip to conquer an unwanted tremor. A girl her size in tears looked as silly as a grownup in a baby bonnet, her sixth grade teacher had once told her.

Michael rubbed a thumb across the peppering of freckles on his nose, leaving a smear of pink jam. "What empty buildings? He said yesterday I could fix up a darkroom in the barn."

"Of course, you can, dear. You go right ahead. Grandpa meant deserted places, ones that have stood empty too long to be safe, not our barn." Aunt Lil dumped a spoonful of sugar into her coffee as she spoke, then a second and a third. "Maybe he got waked up too early this morning, too. He'll be fine in a little while, though. You'll see."

"What did he get so mad about?" Donna asked. She sounded as puzzled and resentful as Annabel felt. "Who was talking about deserted old buildings, anyway? I don't even know where there are any."

"Sure you do, dummy," Todd said. "Haven't you ever been to that old cottage over by Timber Lake? I forget what they call it, but that old house that's supposed to be haunted."

"A haunted house? Really?" Michael's glum face bright-

31

ened. "Where? How come I never heard of it?"

Aunt Lil shook her head at them. "Grandpa said he didn't want to hear anymore about it. I think you'd do a lot better talking about something else."

"How can we be sure we're talking about something else if we don't know what we're talking about now?" Donna asked in a burst of exasperation. "Lost cats, empty buildings, haunted houses, bad jokes— What are we talking about?"

Old Pa uttered a dry sound that could have been a cough or a chuckle. "You're talking about Julia Craig that disappeared over forty years ago without a trace and left folks saying it could have been that the Petersons did her in."

"Pa!" Aunt Lil said quickly. "Your eggs are getting cold."

But she wasn't quick enough to forestall the immediate chorus of "Which Petersons?" from Todd, "Why?" from Donna, and "Not Grandpa!" from Michael.

"It was all nonsense, of course." Aunt Lil's spoon stirred coffee up over the edge of her cup. "Just an empty story started by a lot of loose tongues with nothing better to do. They picked Grandpa and his father, your great-grandpa, for their target, and gave them a pretty unpleasant time for a while. You can't blame Grandpa for not liking to be reminded of it."

Annabel tried to picture Uncle Axel as he might have been forty-odd years ago. If he had the same short temper he'd displayed this morning, she could understand how

32

persons not particularly fond of him could persuade themselves he was capable of violence.

"What does a cat have to do with it?" she asked.

"Well—" Aunt Lil sighed, regarding the four young faces turned to her. "I suppose you won't rest easy until you've heard the whole story."

She drew a deep breath. "Julia Craig was an old maid who taught English at the high school in town. She'd taught there for years, never missed a day, until one Monday morning she didn't show up."

Aunt Lil sipped her super-sweetened coffee, made a face, and carried her cup to the sink to pour the coffee down the drain. "In those days most people who lived any distance out of town didn't have electricity or indoor plumbing yet, and Miss Craig didn't have a phone either. She lived alone in a little house on Timber Lake, so at noon a couple of teachers drove out to see if she was all right."

She refilled her cup and sat down. "They found her car in the shed where she kept it, a bag of groceries on the table, her coat in the closet, and the house in apple-pie order, but the fire was out and the kettle had boiled dry on the stove, and there was no trace of her anywhere. Or her cat. No one ever saw them alive or dead again."

"Maybe they were snatched by aliens from outer space in a flying saucer," Michael suggested, only half in fun.

"Or some kids that hated English," Todd said, transferring another waffle to his plate.

Aunt Lil laughed. "Those are about the only explana-

33

tions nobody thought of, I guess. The sheriff's men searched the house, and there were parties out combing the woods. They even dragged the lake, I remember, although it was frozen nearly halfway across. They never found a clue of any kind, and the place has stood empty ever since."

"Spooky," Donna breathed. "But what made anybody say Grandpa or great-grandpa did something to her? That's dumb."

"Of course it is. But some people will say anything to keep the excitement going a bit longer." Aunt Lil impaled a piece of fried potato on her fork as if it were one of the offenders. "It just happened that your great-grandpa and Miss Craig had words in the post office that Friday, the last day she was ever seen. Her cat was ailing, and she said she wouldn't be surprised if Grandpa or his father had poisoned it. That's all it took for busybodies to start building a mountain out of a molehill."

"They was always having words, the Petersons and Julia Craig," Old Pa told his juice glass. "If it wasn't their dog in her garden, it was her cat in their chickens, or else they was back to fighting over the property line. Then that business about the girl—"

Aunt Lil reached across and gave his plate a brisk quarter turn in front of him. "Eat your eggs, Pa. You haven't touched them."

Old Pa fumbled at his fork and let it lie where it was. "She was a mean one to cross, was Julia Craig. Never forgave nor never forgot. I know. We was classmates together at the old Town Line school. There was a time she had her cap set for Oscar Peterson. Made no bones about it. But he had different ideas and married Jenny Smithfield."

"A good thing he did, too," Aunt Lil said, "or Axel would never have been born and none of us would be sitting here at this table letting good food go to waste."

"What about her grandfather?" Todd asked, waving the syrup pitcher toward Annabel. "If he's Grandpa's brother, where was he when this was happening?"

"He was—" Aunt Lil flicked a glance at Old Pa as if she contemplated spooning eggs into him herself the next time his mouth opened—"living in Chicago already. Now you've heard all there is to tell, so let's get on to something else."

"But is the house really haunted?" Michael persisted, his eyes round and hopeful above a piece of toast. "Which one's the ghost, her or the cat?"

"The cat, naturally." Todd dropped his voice to a stage whisper. "A big gray ghost cat with white markings, name of Macduff."

"Macduff. That's it." Old Pa looked at him and nodded. "She was great on naming things out of books. Macduff. That's what the papers said it was." He nodded again. "Plenty of folks have heard it crying in the woods, and some there are that seen it. She sends it out to lure them to where she's waiting."

A queer little chill crept down Annabel's spine. All three of her cousins were staring at her as if she were some sort of freak, or as if they suspected she had played a joke on them they didn't exactly like.

"I just made it up," she said lamely. "It seemed like a good name."

"Or maybe you heard the story from your grandpa or your father once such a long time ago that you forgot you knew it." Aunt Lil smiled at her. "I'm sure you didn't set out to upset Uncle Axel on purpose."

Annabel returned the smile and chewed down a bite of sausage by way of showing her gratitude. "Anyway, that cat I saw this morning was real. He was no ghost."

That cat that had roamed fluffed and puffed and dry through undergrowth that had drenched her shoes and pants in two steps . . .

Her eyes slid to the window and the dark wall of woods beyond the barn. All the same, wouldn't it be foolish to go blundering off by herself in quest of a cat that might be anywhere by now? More sensible to wait until the poor thing came crying the next time, in case it ever did.

3

Annabel was pleased to find the living room unoccupied when she wandered in after making her bed, one of the few chores required of guests at the farm. The overcast day outside held no appeal for her. Neither did the company of her cousins.

She could hear them calling now and then from the direction of the barn, but she hadn't been asked to join in helping with whatever it was Michael had in mind for creating a darkroom.

Aunt Lil was stirring about in the kitchen, rattling pans and whirring beaters. Uncle Axel was working in the garage.

From Old Pa's room fragments of game shows, soap operas, and comedy reruns were chattering from the TV in irregular spurts as he switched channels at random, even lingering a while on the static buzz of a vacant one, as if they all were the same to him.

Annabel scanned the bookshelves that flanked the big

fireplace on either side. To her delight she spotted a copy of an old friend tucked away in the corner of a top shelf: Sheila Burnford's *The Incredible Journey*.

For the next hour or more she was lost in the wilderness adventures of the Labrador, the bulldog, and the Siamese cat as they trekked their way home across Canada.

When she came up for air at last, she had a much better feeling about the chances of the cat in the Peterson woods.

Also sunshine was pouring in through the windows. And a heavenly fragrance filled the house.

She set her book aside and followed her nose to the kitchen.

Several dozen cookies of assorted kinds were cooling on the newspaper-covered table, and two pans of freshly frosted brownies sat on racks on the counter. Aunt Lil, a chair drawn up to the wall phone and the receiver pressed to her ear, smiled at her and mouthed, "Help yourself."

Annabel selected three of her favorite kind, chocolate chip. Then, rather than stand eating them at the table as if she were listening to Aunt Lil's phone conversation, she strolled on through the back entry and out onto the steps.

A warning yell stopped her in her tracks. Michael hurtled from nowhere to scoop up a camera lying nearly under her foot.

"Hey, Clarabell, what are you doing?" Todd, trailed by Donna, emerged from the side porch. "Can't you watch where you plant those clodhoppers?"

Annabel felt her face redden. "That's a dumb place to leave a camera."

Michael scowled, turning the camera in his hands, examining it for nonexistent damage. "Who knew you were coming with us?"

"Coming where?" Annabel asked.

"Michael—" Donna shot her brother a silencing look and glanced brightly at Annabel. "Where'd you get the cookies?"

Annabel set her jaw. How stupid did they think she was? "Where are you going?"

"She got them from Grandma, naturally," Todd said. "Go get us a bagful to take along, Mike. Tell her we're going for a hike."

Annabel stepped down to let Michael pass, but she kept her eyes fixed on Donna. "A hike where?"

Donna shrugged. "She can come if she wants, can't she?"

Todd mounted the step Annabel had just vacated, a move that brought his face level with hers. "If you can keep your mouth shut about it."

Donna dropped her voice. "We're going to have a look at the haunted house."

A windmill flutter spun inside Annabel. It was as if she had stepped off solid ground into a boggy place where she didn't want to be. "I thought your grandpa told us not to go there."

"He said he didn't want to hear about it." Todd spread his legs, rocking on the heels of the cowboy boots he wore. The embossed black eagles on them reflected his glare. "If he does hear about it, I guess we'll know who told him."

Annabel munched down the last of her cookies without tasting it. She couldn't choose not to go now. They would brand her a goody-goody or chicken.

"It's not that big a deal," Donna said. "We just want to see it. We're not going to hurt anything. You can come or not, whichever you want to."

"Sure. Okay."

Annabel stepped down onto the grass with them, hoping her lack of enthusiasm didn't show. Silly of her not to be ecstatic about receiving so heartfelt an invitation.

Michael pushed out the door, a bulging brown paper bag in one hand, a half-consumed brownie in the other.

"Grandma says for Todd not to get himself overtired," he reported as Todd and Donna dug into the bag.

"Maybe we should take a distress flag to run up in an emergency, seeing as we'll have our own walking flagpole," Todd suggested.

Everyone thought that was funny but Annabel.

She brought up the rear as the hike got underway. Todd, of course, was in the lead. He headed, not for the woods behind the barn as she had somehow expected, but across the yard and straight out to the road. He waved the bag of cookies, now in his possession, on the way past the open garage where his grandfather was filling the gas tank of the lawn mower.

Uncle Axel grinned, including Annabel in his nod: an indication that she was forgiven for the unpleasantness at breakfast.

Annabel found it harder to forgive him. If he could

have shown just a little fairness, if he hadn't been in such a hurry to condemn her out of hand, they would none of them be getting themselves mixed up in this.

Then she wondered where that thought had come from. Mixed up in what? As Donna said, it was no big deal. They weren't going to hurt anything, and nobody really believed in ghosts. Especially not in broad daylight.

So why did it feel like her stomach had gooseflesh for a lining?

Todd was not a fast walker. She had to keep reminding herself to shorten her stride to avoid drifting ahead of him as the procession ambled along the edge of the blacktop road.

"This is the way toward town," Michael objected. "I thought the lake was the other way."

"So what do you want to do? Paint a sign: WE'RE GOING TO THE COTTAGE?" Todd asked.

As soon as the dips and curves of the road hid them from view of the farm, he cut off at an angle into an overgrown meadow.

Donna sidestepped a patch of knee-high thistles. "How far is this cottage?"

"A couple of miles maybe by the road." Todd smacked his lips, polishing off another cookie. "Lucky for you, I know a shorter trail."

He tramped on into the woods at the meadow's far end, and Annabel and the others followed.

It was a minute or two before Annabel realized they actually were on a trail of sorts. Probably it was an old

41

logging trail, and plainly one long unused. The two thinly graveled ruts were nearly obscured by broad-leafed weeds and woody brush growing up between them.

Michael was fingering the camera strap around his neck. "I hope the sun stays out until we get there. I want to get some good pictures."

Todd rolled his pale eyes at the branches overhead. In a raspy whisper he asked, "Why not hope for creepy pictures? Maybe you'll get one of a ghost. Ghosts show up in photographs, you know."

That would be a more unsettling idea, Annabel thought, if lances of sunlight weren't gleaming through the leaves and birds weren't singing everywhere. Or so she told herself.

"I'll tell you what I think is creepy," Donna said. "That's Old Pa. He's like a zombie. I don't see why Grandma wanted to bring him here to live."

"What happened to the little house he had in town?" Michael asked. "I always thought that was kind of neat."

Donna swatted at a mosquito. "It's sold or rented or something, I guess. After he got sick last summer and had to go to the hospital, Grandma said he couldn't live by himself anymore. She could have put him in a nursing home, though, even if he is her father."

"She should have pulled the plug on him while he was in the hospital. I would." Todd stooped to work a long stick free from the underbrush. "If you ask me, he was always a creep. I remember one time me and my folks were up here for Christmas and what's he keep running off at the mouth to me about? How pine needles are flat and firs are pointed or whichever. Wanting to make out he's a big man because he used to work in the woods."

"It's fir needles are flat and pines' are pointed," Annabel murmured. She couldn't resist.

Todd glared at her over his shoulder. "Who made you an expert?"

"I read it in a book." She pulled a tuft of needles from a branch poking out over the trail. "See? These are sharp and they're three-sided. That means they're some kind of pine. They're growing in a bundle, too. Fir needles grow side by side."

Donna and Michael pressed in closer to look. Michael took the needles from her to inspect them more carefully.

"She's right," he marveled. "I never noticed that before."

Todd knocked his stick against a tree root. "Stupendous. Now tell us where Oscar Peterson buried the body, Clarabell."

With a chuckle, Michael tossed the pine needles away and fell into step beside Todd again. "Maybe she can. She knew the name of the ghost cat, remember. What if she's—what do you call it?—psychic?"

"That was an accident, a coincidence," Annabel said hastily, for she wasn't altogether comfortable on that point herself. "I just made up a name to go with M. Our neighbors had a dog once named Macduff."

"Oh, sure, an accidental coincidence. Or maybe you heard it from Old Pa and thought you'd put on a big show." Todd kicked through the twig and leaf debris on the trail, swinging his stick from side to side. "Too bad Old Pa didn't warn you it was our Grandpa's dad that made them into ghosts, the old gal and her cat."

"Hey, watch it!" Donna jumped back as a wild sweep of the stick narrowly missed clipping her ankle.

"You watch it." The stick flattened a fern in the path. "I've got killer blood in me. Smart killer blood. Too smart to get caught. Don't mess with me."

"Grandma didn't say he killed anybody. She said there was talk. Talk doesn't make it true," Donna said from a discreet distance behind him.

"No? What do you think got Grandpa so ticked off this morning? You can bet he believes it's true."

Michael dodged to the side and hauled a birch branch similar to Todd's stick from a tangle of fallen branches. "Did you ever look at that picture by the clock upstairs?" he asked, beginning to whack at the brush, too. "That's Grandpa's father. He sure looks mean enough to kill."

Annabel reflected that he was her grandpa's father, too: that photograph with its tight lips and set jaw and the strange, watching eyes. What secret knowledge lay behind those eyes when the picture was taken? Knowledge beyond the reach now of anyone.

"So would you look mean, probably, if nobody ever believed you," she said, feeling the sting of kindred wounds.

"Because they knew better," Todd insisted. "He was a killer. So am I. Bug me, baby, and you're dead."

His stick demolished a clump of small, perfect trillium. At the cry of protest from Donna and Annabel both, he lurched into a run, beating the foliage to right and left, yelling, "Kill! Kill! Kill!"

Michael charged after him, smashing, trampling, whooping, "Kill! Kill! Kill!"

Annabel knelt beside the broken trilliums. She had seen them in books but never real ones growing wild. Ones that had been growing wild, she corrected herself.

At least the boys were making noise enough that any unwary rabbit or ground-nesting bird or hidden fawn too close to the trail should have ample warning to get out of the way. She had a sickening vision of her cat, Muffin, in the path of a grinning driver chanting, "Kill! Kill! Kill!" as he gunned his engine.

"You guys! Todd! Michael!" Donna's voice did not carry full approval, either. Her indignation slid to a higher pitch as the galloping figures vanished around a bend. "Hey! Wait for us!"

She set off at a run. Annabel did likewise.

On open ground, she could have outdistanced Donna in a few strides and caught up to the boys in not many more. Here in the woods it was different. She was slowed by having to dodge or duck or push aside any number of drooping branches that Donna passed beneath without so much as bowing her head.

Annabel was soon glad of Donna's yellow jeans. They were a patch of light to follow even where the trees shut out the sun entirely, reducing the trail to a dim tunnel.

She knew a moment of panic when the jeans, too, disappeared.

Then the trees thinned, and there was Donna again. She was off the trail, struggling through a thicket of hazel brush toward a sunny opening beyond.

"You guys!" she shouted. "Where are you?"

"Over here," came Michael's voice, echoed by an impatient, "Are you females coming or aren't you?" from Todd.

Todd sounded wheezy, Annabel thought. Perhaps it wasn't smart for a boy with asthma to race around like a mad fiend in the woods.

She wasted no worry on the thought, but scrambled in pursuit of Donna. Extra height was an advantage here. The taller bushes were over Donna's head, but Annabel could see above them and steer a straighter course. Before they gained the clearing where the boys were, Annabel was breaking the way for Donna, and Donna seemed glad to have her do it.

They found Todd seated on a crumbling log, devouring a chocolate chip cookie sandwiched between two of oatmeal.

"Give me a cookie," Donna said. "I need it."

Todd crammed the second half of his sandwich into his mouth and shook his head. "Too late," he said thickly. "All gone." He crumpled the paper bag and tossed it behind the log.

It occurred to Annabel that his wheezing might not be asthma but plain overweight. She turned her eyes from him to Michael. He was performing a peculiar back-and-forth, side-to-side zigzag in the center of the clearing while he squinted into his camera.

She thought at first he was trying for a shot of a dense bush as big as a tree and loaded with purple blossoms. Lilacs this late in the season? Their time was long gone in Chicago before she left home.

But hadn't she read that the advance of spring was delayed a week for every hundred miles north? By that reckoning, it was still May here, not June.

All the same, an ancient lilac alone in a clearing in the Northwoods was an oddity.

Not until she walked on nearly to where Michael was did the house slide into sight.

Annabel halted. She did not know what she had expected: a sinister Victorian mansion, perhaps, with mysterious turrets, sagging balconies, and festoons of moss-grown gingerbread.

What she saw was a simple story-and-a-half cottage of narrow clapboards weathered to dull silver. No turrets. No gingerbread. The closest thing to a balcony was a low porch, which did have a decided outward sag.

The porch steps were gone altogether. So was a sizeable corner of the porch roof. The heavy branch that had done the job lay in a pile of debris below.

Otherwise, except for a broken shutter hanging askew and two or three shattered panes gaping black beside the sheen of intact squares in the windows, the house appeared remarkably untouched by time. A semicircle of pines protected it on every side but the south and the carpet of needles they had laid down over the years had the effect of a recently trimmed if somewhat brownish lawn.

The place was awash in sunlight. Not a sinister shadow anywhere.

"Got it," Michael said with satisfaction. He lowered his camera and started forward.

"This is the haunted house?" Donna sounded disappointed. "I thought it was supposed to be a lake cottage. Where's the lake?"

"It's down behind the trees about half a block." Todd jostled past Annabel and crossed in front of Michael, once more taking the lead.

"Can we get inside, do you think?" Michael asked.

"Sure. Why not? The doors aren't locked."

Donna bounded ahead to walk alongside Todd. "How come you know so much about this place?"

"I came over here with Grandpa and my dad a couple of times one summer and then I came by myself. Grandpa keeps trying to sell the property, but the deal always falls through."

Michael stared around him. "How could Grandpa sell it? Does this belong to him?"

"Naturally. He told me his father bought it for taxes years ago." Todd shrilled a gleeful whinney. "See what I told you? Old Oscar Peterson got rid of the old bag, got her property, and got off scot-free. That's my kind of smart."

He sprinted the remaining distance to the porch and made a clumsy leap up onto it.

Annabel scuffed through the pine needles in silence. She didn't want to go inside. Gooseflesh was beginning to pepper her stomach lining again. Silly, maybe, but real.

Her foot skidded on the slippery needles, and she went down hard on her knee. Twisted ankle, flashed through her mind. Can't go on. Mustn't be moved.

Her cousins didn't stop to see if she was hurt. The three of them were on the porch now, stepping cautiously from one to another of its warped planks.

Todd knocked ostentatiously on the door and gave it a push. It swung in, squealing its reluctance.

Annabel discovered her ankle wasn't twisted. She stumbled to her feet. Much as she didn't want to go inside, she wanted even less to be left behind.

She was on the porch and almost treading on Michael's heels in two jumps.

That same instant, drifting clouds shut out the sun.

4

The ominous dip of rotten wood under Annabel's cautious foot sent her over the doorsill onto sounder flooring in a hasty stride. It was as if the house had given her a little nudge to hurry her inside.

She was in a kitchen. An old-fashioned wood stove squatted against the opposite wall. On another wall, a sink topped by a once-red pump shared space with a mammoth floor-to-ceiling cupboard. Ancient linoleum, robbed of color by dust and time, covered the floor.

"Yuk!" Donna snatched her hand from a rusted teakettle sitting on the stove and wiped a smear of cobwebs off on the seat of her jeans. "If there's a ghost here, it doesn't do housekeeping."

Despite her giggle, her voice was hushed as if, like Annabel, she was troubled by a sense of trespassing where the penalty might be unthinkable if they were caught.

Annabel clasped her hands behind her, wanting to touch nothing.

Michael tugged open one of the glass-paned doors of the cupboard. "What's in here? Just dishes?"

"What's left of them." Todd chuckled. "That summer I first found out about this place, Uncle Jack and his kids, Greg and Chuck, were up here from Florida for a week, and we used these old dishes for target shooting with Chuck's air rifle." His voice was not at all hushed.

"You didn't!" Donna said, shocked. "How do you know they weren't valuable antiques? You might have sold them for a fortune." She pointed to a round oak table by the window. "That's just like the table our mom hunted in about a hundred antique stores to find, and Dad practically had a coronary when he found out how much it cost."

"She could probably have had this one for free," Todd grinned. "Unless maybe the ghost of Julia Craig would have wrestled her for it."

He squinted up at Annabel, smirking. "How about it? Getting any psychic vibes up there, Clarabell?"

"If you're speaking to me," she said icily, "the name is Annabel. Maybe when you get bigger, you'll be able to remember."

She turned her back on him and made a show of going to see what lay beyond a half-open door across the room.

It was a bedroom stripped to its barest essentials. An unadorned dresser of dark wood and a bed, the mattress covered by a drab quilt, were its sole furnishings. Not even a rug on the floor.

"What's this?" Donna asked, peering around Annabel's shoulder. "The spare room?"

"Maybe," Annabel agreed. "It must be she didn't have people overnight very often."

Donna wrinkled her nose. "Grim! I'll bet she served them bread and water if they did come."

Annabel nodded, but the word she would have used was sad rather than grim. She tried to imagine the room as it looked when the stained and peeling paper was an unbroken pattern of rosebuds and ribbons on the wall and the crocheted lace that edged the decaying curtains was fresh and white. Someone once must have taken pains here to make it pretty. Why didn't they finish?

Michael squeezed past her to carry out a drawer-by-drawer inspection of the dresser. "Empty," he reported. "Not even an old sock."

They filed back through the kitchen into the dining room. Here two chairs lay overturned, one of them broken, while two others sat primly upright at the table. A shattered lamp lay in a stain of dust-grimed kerosene on the rag carpet.

"People have been in here rummaging around," Donna said indignantly. "I bet they've walked off with lots of stuff."

"Why not? It's no good just sitting here." Todd scuffed his boot along the seat of a fallen chair to rid the sole of splintered glass. "If Grandpa cared, he'd keep the place locked or else cart the stuff off himself."

Michael snickered, heading for the next room. "But maybe he thinks the ghost of Julia Craig would care."

They were in the front room now, Julia Craig's living

room. Crocheted doilies adorned the arms and backs of two upholstered chairs and a sofa. Tufts of dingy stuffing stuck out of holes in the cushions. Moth holes peppered the carpet.

Annabel's eye was caught by a workbasket beside a high-backed rocking chair. A mother-of-pearl button was skewered to a pincushion by a threaded needle, suggesting the sewer had meant to return shortly with the garment needing repair.

Another basket sat nearby on the windowsill. It was just the right size and the pillow in it dented just the right way to accommodate a curled-up cat. Beneath the layers of dust were there hairs on that pillow of the same silver-gray as the cat in the woods? Macduff?

The sense of trespassing returned like cold fingers on the nape of her neck.

"Hey, look!" Michael snapped a picture of a tall clock on a shelf. "Five twenty-five. I bet it stopped the hour Julia Craig disappeared."

"Why not, if she never came back to wind it? You don't think it would keep running by itself forever, do you?" Todd scoffed.

Michael covered his chagrin by starting for the clock. "I wonder if it still runs."

"No, don't!" The words escaped Annabel before she could think. She couldn't have told what her objection was, except for a premonition that to rouse the old clock would be a mistake.

"Don't touch it," Donna echoed her. "The thing's filthy

with cobwebs and probably full of spiders besides. Leave it alone, Michael."

She opened the door to an adjoining room. "Oh, look! Here's the real bedroom. Clothes and books and everything."

Their attention was diverted from the clock immediately. Todd and Michael crowded in ahead of Annabel, but she had a clear view over their heads of a neatly made bed, a checkered apron folded over a chair, a painting of a mountain village in winter on the wall.

Curiosity drew her to the dresser. A pair of black cotton gloves, neatly darned, lay alongside two hairbrushes, a comb, and a lacquer box containing big, bone-colored hairpins.

Pins for gray hair or blonde, Annabel wondered? What had Julia Craig looked like? Was it her personality or lack of beauty that had turned Great-grandpa Oscar off?

Michael pulled a manila envelope out of a bookshelf. "Hey, neat! Old snapshots. And negatives," he said, pulling out a handful to examine by the window. "This is my kind of stuff."

Annabel followed to bend over his shoulder as he began shuffling through his find. Strange to think if one were of Julia Craig, they wouldn't know how to recognize her.

"Lots of clothes in here," Donna announced, lifting a yellowed cotton slip from a drawer. "Wait, what's—?"

She broke off with a shriek and leaped backward into Annabel's arms. They crashed together into Michael, clutching each other partly for balance and partly in panic.

"It moved," Donna gasped. "I saw something move."

Todd shot a burst of profanity at them. "Just a mouse nest." He scooped a pile of folded clothing from the drawer and strode out. "I'll take care of them."

The thin squeaks of baby mice brought Annabel to her senses. "No! Wait! Don't!" she cried after him.

Her rush to unscramble herself from Donna and Michael sent her tumbling over the chair and lost her precious time. She got no farther than the front room before the tread of Todd's boots returning proclaimed his mission accomplished.

"What did you do with them?" she demanded.

He flexed his shoulders carelessly. "Took them out and stepped on them. What else?"

She fought back an urge to throw up. "You could have left them where they were. They weren't doing you any harm."

"Oh, wow!" Todd groaned. "Don't tell me we've got a Bambi lover." He struck a pose, hands clasped and eyes rolled heavenward. "Animals is weally sweet wittle people in fur coats, and we should wuv them wike brothers."

"Their lives are as important to them as yours is to you," she said hotly.

He laughed. "No way." And then he wasn't clowning anymore. "Listen, Clarabell. Just because you're built like an ox, don't get the idea you swing any weight around here. If our way don't grab you, there's nothing says we'll miss you if you split."

She shouldn't let herself be hurt by such crudities, but

even while her fingers twitched to shake him by the collar of his fancy Western shirt, the retort she ought to spit at him wedged crosswise in her throat. "Thanks. I'm glad to," was the best she could manage.

She snatched at a door she supposed led outside. Instead, she found herself at the foot of a flight of stairs.

The mockery in Todd's laugh drove her on up them two at a stride without a second thought.

Before she gained the top, she was stooping almost double beneath the slope of the roof. No one above five feet tall could have done otherwise.

She was in the attic. To get to where she could stand without hitting her head on a rafter, she had to cross nearly a third of the rough plank floor.

Dust thick as a carpet muted her footsteps. Queer how the brooding quiet of this house made her want to tiptoe. As if she feared to wake someone. Or something.

Her breath stopped as a flicker of movement caught her eye. But it was only herself, a girl with tumbled dark hair and a sunburned nose, reflected in a murky mirror that leaned against the chimney.

The place held the usual attic clutter of boxes, discarded bric-a-brac, and oddments of furniture. Two wide bookcases of brick-and-plank construction stood shoulder to shoulder beside the thick stone column of the chimney, one of them lower than the other to accommodate the slope of the roof. What was perhaps a wardrobe, its back side to the room for some reason, filled the remaining space between them and the outer wall. The dust of decades lay undisturbed on everything.

Annabel had no intention of lingering up here, but she hesitated to go down while Todd might still be watching to jeer at her mistake. Maybe it would do no harm to spend a minute reading some of the titles that crowded the bookshelves.

The sun had broken through the clouds again. It laid an inviting beam, almost cheerful, across a section of the books by way of a small gable window.

She tiptoed nearer a row of faded spines, prepared to discover—what? Tomes on black magic, perhaps, or dark philosophies? Certainly anything but the well-worn old acquaintances that met her eye: *A Child's Garden of Verses, Winnie-the-Pooh, The House at Pooh Corner, Raggedy Ann & Andy*—a whole series of those—*The Secret Garden, Black Beauty, The Five Little Peppers, Little Lord Fauntleroy*. And dozens more.

This was a child's library, and one that showed the signs of having been much read. How did this fit into the picture of the embittered old-maid schoolteacher that was Julia Craig?

Many of these books Annabel had read. Others she had heard of but never happened on, like *The Blue Fairy Book*, nestled here between *Tom Sawyer* and *Little Women*. Poor thing, it wasn't blue anymore but a nondescript gray.

Annabel squatted on her heels for a closer view, her instinct strong as ever to touch nothing, to leave as little imprint of herself as possible in this house. How then the book got from the shelf into her hand she was never sure. It was just there.

The pages flipped open by themselves as if eager to be read again. *". . . for within an hour's time there grew up all round the park such a vast number of trees and small bushes and brambles twining one within another, neither man nor beast could pass through."*

She read on, intrigued to discover that in this book the mother of Sleeping Beauty's prince ate little children.

"Hey, Clarabell!" Todd's jeer from below scraped her nerves like sandpaper. "We're going, Clarabell. Bye-bye, Clarabell."

She sprang up, slamming the book shut. Anger swept away her qualms about disrupting the quiet.

"The name is ANNABEL!" She emptied her lungs into the shout. "Annabel Lee Peterson!"

There was a sudden stillness. Even the dust motes lazily afloat in the sunlight froze where they were. It was like the breath-holding instant before a thunderclap.

But there was no thunder. Only a soft, drawn-out sigh. It could have been the old house settling, except that it sounded like a whispery echo: "Ann-nie . . ."

I stood up too fast, I shouted too hard, she tried to tell herself. But something fundamental in her knew that wasn't the answer. Knew it before she saw the suspended motes begin to revolve, spiraling more dust up into a miniature whirlwind that thickened and grew. And advanced.

For a second she couldn't move. When she did wrench her legs into action, the stairway seemed to have receded a hundred yards. She hardly felt the low beam that grazed her head as she hurled herself down the steps.

The door at the bottom stood open. She banged it shut behind her and fled on through the parlor, the dining room, into the kitchen. There she had to stop for breath.

Todd, Donna, Michael, where were they? The door to the porch, left open while they were in the house, was closed now.

And someone had set the old clock going in the parlor after all. Its measured ticking reached through the house, waking faint stirrings where there had been only musty silence. A tendril of hair fluttered against her damp temple, and the ancient curtains at the windows billowed briefly in the dead air.

She seized the doorknob. It turned loosely in her grip without budging the door.

In the depths of the house, another latch clicked and hinges creaked. The attic door?

She grasped the knob in both hands and yanked. It pulled off in her fist, dragging the door inward a bare crack.

"Annie." The whisper sighed around her again. Not the shifting of sagging beams. A breathy, questing whisper. *"Ann—nie."*

Annabel dug her nails into the edge of the door and tore it open. The rotted sill gave way under her foot. Her heel plunged ankle-deep into a trap of jagged splinters as the house—the presence in the house—sought one last means to hold her.

Her sneaker was left still a prisoner as she jerked free. She didn't stay to rescue it.

The whisper—anguished, angry, appealing—pursued her across the pine-needle yard, past the laden lilac tree: *"A-a-ann-nie!"*

She lurched on at a limping run in one stocking foot and one sneaker until she could hear nothing but her own gasping for breath. The hazel thicket rose before her, promising the logging trail and the way out of the woods. There was the log Todd had sat on, the discarded paper bag that had held cookies.

"Donna?" she called. "Michael?"

Please, let them come bursting out of hiding to tell her she was the butt of a nasty joke. She wouldn't mind their laughter, would welcome their jeers.

"Todd?"

No one answered, and she didn't wait to call again. Panting, she pushed into the thicket.

It was harder to steer a straight course going back than it had been with a clearing ahead to aim for. The brush was higher than she remembered, the branches thicker and more resolutely crisscrossed in a wickerwork that all but defied passage.

Neither did she recall there had been so many mosquitoes earlier. They swarmed around her. The air fairly shimmered with tiny, moving bodies. Their mean, high whine was everywhere. She brushed a cluster of them from the side of her face, and was surprised to feel a sticky welt above her temple. A smear of dark blood came away on her fingers. For the first time she realized there was a throbbing ache where she had struck her head in her flight from the attic.

The memory spurred her to struggle against the walling greenery more frantically than before. At last she fought through to the trail. But the trail, too, had changed. Was it this faint, this narrow, this thickly overgrown an hour ago?

Pine boughs raked her hair like coarse combs, pulling, snarling it. Squadrons of mosquitoes launched themselves from beneath stands of fern to attack her shoeless foot. Sapling wands grew in the path and snapped back like whips when she bent them out of the way. Still she forged desperately on until a clump of birch—five big trunks growing tightly together—blocked the track completely. She knew beyond question that she had passed no such barrier when she came.

Steady down. Don't panic, she told the wild thudding in her chest. *So you mistook a deer track or something for the trail. Just follow it back and start over.*

But when she turned to retrace her steps, the path was gone. Nowhere in the undergrowth was there a break that appeared to lead anywhere. In the direction she was about to choose, loops of thorny blackberry vines fenced her off as effectively as barbed wire.

That line from the fairy-tale book slid into her mind: ". . . *within an hour's time there grew up all round the park such a vast number of trees and small bushes and brambles twining one within another . . ."* That fairy tale in which the old queen ate young people for dinner.

Annabel set her teeth in her lower lip to control it. *I won't panic. It's not like I'm lost in a trackless wilderness. The farm can't be too far away. Aunt Lil and Uncle Axel will be out hunting for me the minute I turn up missing.*

There! She stiffened, listening. Was that a distant voice shouting her name? Shouting: "Annabel?" Or was it—she held her breath to hear—a voice calling: *"Ann-nie?"*

Annabel whirled and bolted in the opposite direction.

She had no idea how far she ran, nor how long, nor when it began to rain. The patter of raindrops on leaves had been going on almost forever when exhaustion dropped her at last onto a water-slicked rock the size of a tabletop. With a shiver, she saw it was very like a rock she had passed a little while ago. She thought of her fancy that the cat this morning was compelled by some baleful enchantment to wander in an endless circle that never quite let him escape these woods.

Hang onto your wits; don't panic, she reminded herself. *You're too big to cry.*

A dog howled somewhere at no great distance, and she shrank into a heap of knotted arms and drawn-up legs. The next instant she was on her feet. Where there was a dog, there would probably be people.

Please, dog, keep howling, she begged silently as she stumbled over tree roots and around deadfalls, following the sound. *Don't anyone shut him up or chase him away!* She could almost believe it was Ricky, howling as he was inclined to do when someone hooked him on his chain. But that would be too good to be true.

Yet it was true. Incredibly, as she climbed the top of a slope, she glimpsed the barn ahead through the trees. She lost sight of it on the downward side of the slope, but that didn't matter. She knew now where she was going.

If she could get there. All at once she was surrounded by blackberry brambles. Wicked thorns caught hold of her jeans. Others stabbed the heel of her unprotected foot when she tried to back off. She couldn't go forward or to either side. It was then that she heard the cat cry behind her.

Annabel screamed. "Help! Somebody, please! Help!"

"That you, girl?" came the answer from close-by. "Over here. Come this way."

She lunged, heedless of the briars, and somehow the barrier melted away, becoming a jumble of harmless weed stalks and seedling pines.

Then she was clear of the woods and clinging to Old Pa, who wrapped her in arms surprisingly strong for all that they trembled slightly. She pressed her face against his rain-soaked sweater, oblivious to how silly it looked for big girls to cry, while Ricky, cringing at the farthest limit of his chain, continued to howl dismally at the trees.

5

Annabel woke the next morning to the singing of birds outside the window and a breath of flower fragrance on the air.

She lay still, hanging onto drowsiness, not wanting to wake up all the way. There was something she would have to remember if she did, something she dreaded remembering.

Muffin is dead. Her mind touched the familiar pain almost as a reassurance that there was nothing else.

Then there was a rustle somewhere in the room. Recollection burst on her, jerking her up on her elbow. Her throat knotted shut against a scream.

"Sorry," Donna said, comb in hand in front of the mirror. "Did I wake you up? I was trying to be so quiet."

Annabel sat up the rest of the way more slowly. Her heartbeat leveled off as she took in details of the airy bedroom, bright with summer light.

"That's okay." She blinked at Donna's bed, made up

neat and smooth as if it had never been slept in. "What time is it?"

"About nine-thirty. A little after. Grandma said to let you sleep as late as you could." Donna regarded her curiously. "How's your head today?"

Annabel raised a hand to the welt on the side of her head. "It's all right. Sore, but not too bad." She pushed off the bedclothes and stood up.

"I'm fine," she said testily, aware that Donna was watching her. "There's nothing wrong with me."

"Sure." Donna turned back to the mirror and became busy flipping up the ends of her hair. "It's a really nice day out. We're going to bike into town so Michael can get some stuff he needs for developing pictures. Want to come along?"

"I don't know," Annabel said, knowing very well. She reached for her terry-cloth robe. "Probably not. I'm going to go wash up. Anybody in the bathroom right now?"

Donna shook her head. "Not when I came up." She went on staring into the mirror until Annabel was almost through the door. Then, speaking to her comb, she said in a rush, "We did wait for you yesterday. When you didn't come, we thought you were just mad at us. But we did wait a while, whatever you think."

They had waited for ten minutes, according to Todd's virtuous account when the cousins were called on for their version of the day's events. At a later telling it had become twenty minutes, and by last night he was certain they'd waited half an hour at the very least.

Annabel felt a pulse throb in her bruised temple. "I should believe you, but you don't have to believe me."

"I never said I don't believe you." Donna turned pink. "I mean I believe it when you say you aren't making any of it up, but— Well, like Grandma says—"

"Right. I knocked myself silly and saw ghosts instead of stars," Annabel finished for her.

That was the explanation they had settled on, Aunt Lil and the rest of them: the blow to Annabel's head had scrambled her wits for a time. Not for a moment had anyone but Old Pa behaved as if there were the smallest possibility that what she had seen and heard were real.

Donna eyed her unhappily. "We did wait for you," she repeated, sounding as if she would gladly have said anything else if she could.

"Okay," Annabel conceded with a sigh. Whatever had happened yesterday, Donna was trying to say she was sorry. That should count for something. "Anyhow, it's over now. Let's forget about it."

But, of course, what Donna was sorry for was Annabel herself. Poor Annabel, who was even freakier than the cousins had thought her at the start.

She and Donna traded wary smiles, and Annabel retreated to the privacy of the bathroom and a steamy shower.

When at last she came downstairs, the chug of the washer in the basement and the mutter of TV from Old Pa's room gave her hope that she had dawdled long enough for everyone to be gone off about their own affairs and not waiting for her. She wasn't keen on fielding more stares and questions right away.

But there in the kitchen, scrubbing grease from his hands, was Uncle Axel. Neither he nor Annabel smiled on seeing one another.

She had been in such a state yesterday that even he had been at pains to soothe her, but she hadn't scored any points with him by rousing the ghost of Julia Craig, let alone making such an issue of it.

Annabel opened the refrigerator, and spoke from within the shelter of its door. "Good morning."

"Morning." He shut off the water and began drying his hands on the towel beside the sink. After a moment, he cleared his throat. "I've been cleaning up the old bikes in the garage. The kids took off on three of them a while ago, but there's still a couple you can choose from if you want to."

"Thank you." Annabel pulled out the orange juice. "Only I think I'll call my mom before anything else. I'll reverse the charges."

"Never mind about the charges." The stern lines relaxed a bit around his mouth. "I suspect we can absorb those without too much strain."

Did he guess the purpose of her call? she wondered as she watched him go out the back door. If so, he doubtless counted it cheap at triple the price, for she meant to tell her mother she was coming home.

The fact was she would be on her way already if her

mother had seen fit to be home last night to answer the phone. And if Aunt Lil hadn't put her out of business finally with one of Old Pa's "mild" tranquilizers.

That was an odd thing, her mother's not being home, for Friday was her night to climb into old clothes, put her feet up, and unwind.

Annabel set a glass on the counter. As she tilted the juice bottle over it, there came a thud and rattling crash somewhere inside the house. Orange juice splashed everywhere but into her glass.

"What was that?" Aunt Lil yelled from the basement. "Who's in the kitchen?"

"Me. Annabel." She hoped her voice wasn't as shaky as her hands. So much for the benefits of tranquilizers and a good night's sleep.

Aunt Lil burst up out of the basement. "What happened?"

"It was that way." Annabel pointed. "Maybe the living room."

Aunt Lil set off at a trot, Annabel on her heels.

What they found was Old Pa standing in the front hall closet, a jumble of fallen boxes, umbrellas, hats, and tennis racquets on the floor at his feet. He was probing a long arm among what articles remained on the closet shelf.

"Pa! What on earth do you think you're doing?" Aunt Lil demanded.

"My box," he said irritably. "My tackle box. I can't find it."

"I don't know what you're talking about, Pa. Look what

you've done." Aunt Lil pulled a flashlight from the heap and snapped it on experimentally. "It's a miracle this still works."

Old Pa continued his rummaging. "My compass is in that box. I want to find my compass."

"Well, I can assure you it's not here. It's in your room if it's anywhere." Aunt Lil nudged him aside and began restoring order to the shelf with a briskness nearly as violent as the crash.

Annabel saw bewilderment clouding the old man's face. "A green tackle box. I always keep it in the hall closet."

"That was at your house, not this one," Aunt Lil said, nodding thanks to Annabel for handing an umbrella up to her. "Anything of yours is in your room. If not, maybe it's something we decided not to bring along. We couldn't bring everything you had in that house."

Old Pa rubbed the gray stubble on his chin. "You decided," he muttered. "Not me. Nobody asked me."

"Now, Pa, you're lucky to have a family that looks after you. You'd be in a fine fix if nobody cared what became of you."

The sulky hunch of Old Pa's shoulders suggested to Annabel that he didn't consider his luck an unmixed blessing.

She could understand his feeling, for she had been "looked after" herself to the point of suffocation yesterday. Aunt Lil had soothed her with glasses of hot milk and cups of sweetened tea enough to float a yacht, had pressed ice cubes and cold compresses to the lump on her head, patted meat tenderizer on her mosquito bites, painted antiseptic on her scratches, phoned the clinic in town to make sure her condition didn't indicate concussion, and at last had administered that pill which had put Annabel to sleep almost before she could stumble into bed. All this done with such an anxious bustle that it was like being battered to death by pillows.

Annabel eased herself back to the kitchen while Aunt Lil was still too busy with Old Pa to remember to be solicitous about her again. As a sort of apology, she grabbed a handful of paper towels and mopped up the spilled orange juice. Aunt Lil's heart really was in the right place even if she did come on pretty strong.

But that didn't change a thing. Annabel had had her fill of this farm and all that went with it. She lifted the kitchen phone from its hook and started the dial whirring: 1 for long distance, 312 for Chicago . . .

The phone at the other end began to ring. It rang and rang and rang—as it had last night when no one answered.

She waited, swallowing down a crazy fancy that she might be trapped here in a twilight zone where the ringing was only a sound in space and there were no other phones to connect with anymore.

Then there was a click, and a voice barely recognizable as her mother's croaked, "Hello?"

"Mom? Is that you?"

"Annabel!" Surprise cleared away some of the hoarseness. "Of course it's me. I'm just not quite awake yet."

"You mean I woke you?" Annabel shot a glance at the clock above the sink. "How come? It's going on eleven. Are you sick or something?"

Beneath her dismay there was an undeniable leap of hope. If her mother were ill, she would need Annabel at home. Immediately!

"No, I'm fine. I got to bed too late last night, that's all." Her mother was sounding more like herself by the moment. "But I wasn't looking for a call from you today. I thought we were going to phone on Sundays."

Suspicion pushed ahead of Annabel's yearning to pour out her woes. "Who kept you up so late? Donald?"

"Well, yes." There was the faintest shade of reluctance in her mother's answer. Perhaps even guilt, Annabel thought. "Donald and some friends of his. Another couple. We went out to dinner and afterward a play."

Annabel didn't miss the reference to "another" couple. Was her mother beginning to think of Donald and herself as a couple, too? A pair who belonged together?

Annabel's fist clamped harder on the receiver. "He doesn't lose any time, does he? I mean, my bed's hardly cold and there he is, taking over."

"Don't let's get started on that nonsense." Her mother's voice sharpened. "Nobody's taking over anything, least of all your place. And nobody wants to. Donald's as much your friend as he is mine, or he would be if you'd give him half the chance."

Annabel glared at a blue flower in the tiled wall. "Sure."

"Annabel—" Her mother's exasperation trailed off in

futility. "You haven't said why you're calling. Is anything wrong?"

"Just me, I guess. I thought you'd be getting kind of lonesome. I made a mistake, I guess."

"I am lonesome. I miss you. But we've got to get used to being apart some of the time. I can't expect to hang onto you forever."

That was Donald's talk. Her mother hadn't worried about hanging on before he butted in.

"What's the matter, honey?" her mother asked when Annabel said nothing. "Aren't you having a good time?"

The tile flower blurred. Annabel ached to spill out the truth of her terror and homesickness. But the swell of anger in her chest wouldn't let the words get by. She squeezed out a thin, "Not very."

"Oh, honey," her mother said. "But you've only been there a few days. I know it's hard the first time away from home, but it's bound to get better."

"Is it?"

Her mother paused. "Listen—I wasn't going to mention this just yet because it may not work out, but maybe I can be up there with you for the Fourth of July weekend. Donald thinks he can get away for four days then, and if so, we'll drive up there. Would you like that?"

The Fourth of July. That was eons away. And Donald again. Donald, always Donald. "Super," Annabel said through set teeth.

"Honey, something is the matter. I can tell. What is it?"

Annabel gathered in a breath that cut like wire. "Nothing. Nothing I can't handle by myself."

It wasn't a decision. It was a reflex, like hitting back at someone who hurt you. But once spoken, it couldn't be unsaid.

After the receiver was back on its hook, Annabel stood a while, absorbing the impact of what she had done. She was stuck here now, committed to facing down the nightmares, the ridicule, the loneliness of being the weirdo outsider, all on her own.

Shock gradually boiled into anger. Blast Donald Kimball! Wouldn't he be pleased at the way she'd trapped herself because of him?

Well, if she said she could handle things here, then handle them she would. Somehow.

Head up and shoulders squared, she slammed out the back door. At least she could grab a bike and get away from here for a while.

A Morning Glory milk truck was swinging into the drive as she cut across between the house and the garage. Ricky hurtled from nowhere, threatening to attack it, but a command from Uncle Axel inside the garage silenced him.

"It's all right. His bark is all there is to that dog," Aunt Lil called from the front porch. Then as the driver rather gingerly stepped out of the truck, "Sue, for goodness sake! You don't look much like our milkman. Where's your dad?"

The young woman in coveralls laughed. "Dad's been

short a driver lately, so I sort of got drafted. You never know what teachers will end up doing for the summer."

"Pa," Aunt Lil said over her shoulder, "you remember Sue Gordon, don't you? You and her grandma used to be schoolmates, I think. Mrs. Gordon, Dr. Gordon's wife."

"Ethel Briggs before she was married," Sue supplied when Old Pa made no answer. "How are you, Mr. Schulty? Grandma will be glad to hear I saw you."

Annabel, hesitating near the corner of the house, blinked up at the porch. Mr. Schulty? It hadn't occurred to her that Old Pa must have a real name like anyone else.

"How is your grandma?" Aunt Lil asked, descending the steps to help carry in the milk. "I heard you'd moved her into one of those new apartments across from the clinic."

"She moved herself. Put her name in for the apartment, made the arrangements, and told us how we should help." Sue shook her head, grinning. "You'd never guess she'll be ninety-three in August. Her mind's sharp as a tack. She even goes over my newspaper columns for me and catches me off base on grammar and spelling more times than I like to admit."

"You do a wonderful job with that column," Aunt Lil said. "It's the first thing I turn to every week when the *North Star Shopper* comes out. I don't know how you find so many interesting stories about things that happened around here."

Sue was scanning the order list. "I do some tall scrounging at times. And Grandma's memory's sent me off on some great leads."

Old Pa shuffled forward, leaning on his cane. "Tell your grandma Julia's stirring."

Sue straightened, a milk carton in each hand. "Do what?"

"Tell Ethel that Julia Craig's stirring again. She'll know what you're saying."

Aunt Lil slid a laugh in ahead of the chance of another question, but Annabel didn't wait to learn whether that ended the discussion. If there was any topic she could do without at present, it was Julia Craig.

She faded back along the garage, and dodged in through the side door.

"Either of these bikes okay for me to ride?" she asked Uncle Axel, who was arranging tools on a pegboard above his workbench. "I just want to ride along the road, not go anywhere special."

He nodded. "Stick to the blacktop and I guess you won't get lost."

He probably meant it kindly, but it was a pointed reminder that she hadn't exactly distinguished herself in any respect yesterday.

Smarting worse than ever at the unfairness of it all, she picked a battered but sturdy-looking four-speed and pedaled down the drive in the wake of the departing milk truck. At the road, because the truck turned left, she veered right. Too late, she realized that her choice was the same route Todd had led them on yesterday. Her mouth went a little dry but pride wouldn't let her turn back.

She recognized the overgrown pasture they had waded through, and at its farther side the stretch of woods enclosing that elusive logging trail. There was nothing to see today but white daisies dotting the tall grass, nothing to hear but birds singing among the trees. Nothing to hint that anything sinister might lurk beyond.

All right, Julia Craig, she challenged silently. You had your inning. Now it's a whole new ball game. Annabel Lee Peterson is up to bat.

The pasture remained tranquil under a cloudless sky. Soon it was swept from view by a curve of the road and a sun-dappled archway of maples.

Half a mile farther on civilization started to thrust into the landscape. She passed a trailer court, an outdoor movie theater, and a handful of modest houses set back from the road, one with a sign atop its mailbox offering fresh eggs for sale.

More woods, another open field, and a chain link fence surrounding a small cemetery.

Annabel slowed the bike, intrigued by the jumble of different headstones—some slim pinnacles, some massive blocks, some sculptured into praying hands or life-size angels. This must be an old place. Where her father was buried, the graves were marked by identical metal plates, very neat and very monotonous.

The gate was open, practically an invitation to come in and have a closer look. She leaned the bike against the gatepost and walked uphill along a gravel path.

What a lot of stories the old stones could tell. Here were three small ones in a row in a family plot: George, William, and Grace. Three children who had died within a week of each other seventy years ago.

And here, carved on one end of a long granite rectangle, was Dr. Eugene Gordon, 1885–1962. The second half read: Ethel B. Gordon, 1890–19—. Old Pa's friend, that must be.

Think of knowing that your tombstone was waiting for you, year after year, all but the final two digits of the date.

And yet, when Annabel thought about it, wasn't it like a pledge of faithfulness and love for a wife to link herself to her husband like that for eternity? There was no such unfinished marker bearing her mother's name.

Annabel drifted on up the path, noting how some plots looked freshly tended and others as if they hadn't been visited in decades. On one of these, a square, gray stone was just visible through the high weeds around it. She pushed aside a thistle with her foot to see the inscription.

The weathered numbers were visible first: 1891–19—. Someone else whose final resting place was still waiting.

She bent the thistle farther to reveal the name.

Julia Craig.

Annabel's spring backward landed her on the path in a flurry of gravel before the released thistle stopped swaying. Also before her wits caught up with her. Of course the stone was unfinished, for Julia Craig, whatever her intentions, never got here. In fact, this was one place a person need have no fear of meeting her.

Annabel nearly laughed aloud as she turned away. Nice try, Julia, but you missed me.

Sunlight struck somber sparkles from a similar gray stone in the plot opposite. The grass had been roughly trimmed away here, and the lines cut into the stone were rain-washed clean of debris.

The name leaped up at her: ANNABEL LEE PETERSON.

6

"Your grandmother? Yes, of course, that's what she'd be," Aunt Lil nodded, stacking lunch dishes in the dishwasher. "Your father's mother. It's hard to picture her a grandmother, she was so young."

"Nineteen," Annabel supplied. The dates beside the name on the stone—1920–1939—were what had given her the clue to who the Annabel in the grave must be. No need to rehash the stupid fantasies that had paralyzed her before the answer came.

She screwed the lid on the pickles and set the jar in the refrigerator. Helping Aunt Lil clear up after lunch provided an opportunity to ask questions without interference—humorous or otherwise—from the sidelines. Uncle Axel was off to his puttering in the garage again, Old Pa to take a nap, Donna to try on the finery she had bought in town, Michael and Todd to the barn with Michael's darkroom supplies.

"I knew she died when my father was born," Annabel

continued to Aunt Lil's bent back, "but I didn't know she was so young. And I didn't know she was buried here. I thought it all happened in Chicago."

"Well, yes, it did. But her home was up here. I suppose maybe Walter, your grandpa, thought it was fitting to bring her back for burial, although he hasn't been back himself but twice since, that I know of—once to his mother's funeral and again to his father's."

"She was from around here? My grandmother, I mean?" It struck Annabel that she knew next to nothing about this grandmother. She had never even seen a picture of her. "Did you know her?"

"Yes, some. But there was several years' difference in our ages. I had my teacher's certificate already, and was finishing up my first year of teaching over in Melville and she was still a high school student when they ran off."

"When who ran off? My grandmother?" Annabel forgot she was trying to sound casual.

Aunt Lil pulled her head out from under the sink and straightened, a box of detergent in her hand. "She and Walter. They eloped the day after she turned eighteen. Nobody had a clue to where they'd gone until your father was well on the way and it was too late to have the marriage annulled."

Aunt Lil sighed, measuring detergent into the dishwasher. "Poor kids. A lot of good it did them. It lacked a week of her next birthday the day of her funeral. I remember that."

Annabel sponged away the catsup smears on the plastic place mat that had been under Todd's plate. Her Grandpa Peterson part of a tragic romance? Incredible.

He lived in New Mexico now, and she hadn't seen him in three years. Neither had she missed him much, anymore than he probably did her.

It wasn't that he was unkind or uncaring, but his efforts to show a grandfatherly interest in what she liked and what she did were always just that: efforts.

He had a way of looking at her sometimes when she was playing or reading or merely crossing the room, as if what he saw gave him more pain than pleasure. She wondered now had he been comparing her—gawky, oversized, bookish—to that other Annabel, who was— what?

"Why did they elope?" A baby born a full year later obviously ruled that out as a reason. "What was wrong that they couldn't get married at home?"

"Oh, various things, I suppose," Aunt Lil said, growing vague. She set the controls of the dishwasher and turned it on. "Can you reach that big green dish down from the cupboard above the refrigerator? I think I'll make potato salad for supper, and that will about hold enough for all of us."

Annabel wasn't to be put off that easily. "Various things like what?" she persisted over the rumble of the dishwasher. "Wasn't Grandpa good enough for her parents or something?"

"She didn't have any parents. Not living ones. She lived with—" Aunt Lil paused, watching her lift down the dish— "a relative. Thank you, dear. You are a handy helper. I'd have had to drag out the step stool."

For once Annabel ignored a reference to her height. "Are any relatives still living around here?"

Not that she was burning to acquire more cousins, goodness knew, but she was eager to scan every page in this unsuspected chapter in her family history.

Aunt Lil shook her head. "They're gone, all of them. All dead. But look here." She produced a foil-wrapped packet from the breadbox. "Two brownies left from yesterday. Why don't you have yourself a treat out in the sunshine? You've earned it."

Which meant that the subject of Annabel's grandmother was exhausted as far as Aunt Lil was concerned.

Annabel took the hint and the brownies, although she wasn't particularly hungry and she could think of a dozen more questions to ask. Adults had an annoying habit of telling only selected parts of a story and letting it go at that.

Uncle Axel was backing his jeep down the drive when she came out onto the front porch. He was too occupied watching the road to notice her, which was just as well. At least when he asked during lunch if she had reached her mother, he had refrained from groaning like Todd on learning that she would be staying on at the farm as long as originally planned. At any rate, through the Fourth of July.

She sat down on the porch steps, choosing not to count up how many weeks and days lay between now and the Fourth.

She had neglected to mention Julia Craig's tombstone to Aunt Lil. Accidentally or on purpose? She wasn't sure. And Aunt Lil, who surely knew it was there, had understandably neglected to speak of it, either.

Annabel shivered and stretched her legs into a patch of sun, turning her mind again to the other Annabel.

She must have been miserable here, too. Even supposing Grandpa Peterson to have been devastating in his youth—which was supposing a lot—cutting herself off from family and home forever seemed a drastic step to take.

Ricky, his lopsided tail beating his side hopefully, thrust his broad head into Annabel's lap, nudging the packet of brownies. Well, why not? She opened the foil and fed them both to him.

It did queer things to her stomach to think of being uprooted in any way, much less of inviting changes that didn't need to be. There were changes enough that came without invitation. Fathers died; pets got killed; legs added unwanted inches every year; mothers became strangers overnight, dancing to whatever tune some phony charm boy chose to whistle.

Annabel crushed the foil into a ball, all her anger of the morning flooding back. They couldn't keep her tucked away in Wisconsin forever, Donald and her mother. And once she got home, their party would be over. She could promise them that.

Ricky flinched from her half-lifted fist as if he expected a blow.

"Sorry, boy. I didn't mean you." She opened her hand and extended it to him as a peace gesture.

Ricky, however, was not a dog to place much trust in empty gestures. Not until she thought to uncrumple the foil and hold it so he could lick the smudges of frosting from it did his tail begin to wag again.

"That you, girl?" Old Pa asked, letting the screen door bang behind him as he crossed the porch.

"It's me. Annabel." She folded the now frosting-free foil into a small square and stuffed it in her jeans pocket to throw away later. Uncle Axel had already spoken sharply to Todd about a 7-Up can left by the hammock and directed Michael's attention to the garbage can as the proper receptacle for gum wrappers. Littering his velvet lawn was one charge he wasn't going to have against her.

"Annabel. Yes," Old Pa said, as if for once the name really registered. "Here, I want you to have this."

She twisted around to see that he was holding out a tarnished brass case the size of a pocket watch. "What is it?" she asked, standing up for a better look.

"Compass. I thought they'd thrown it out with the rest of my things, but I found it." The lid of the case sprang up to reveal a lightly swinging needle. "I carried this a good many years, all the time I worked in the woods. Never failed me once." He rocked it gently in his palm. "You know how to use a compass?"

"I know the needle always points north," Annabel said doubtfully.

"That's a start." He eased himself onto the porch swing and beckoned her to sit beside him. "Here, I'll show you."

Annabel sat down without the least intention of ever straying far enough again to want a compass.

"First thing, you want to keep the needle always pointed North. What I mean is, pointing to this here big N." He tilted the case so she could watch the needle swing to rest on the N, pointing almost directly at the back of the swing. His finger tapped the S at the needle's rounded end. "So now you know you're facing south. See? You got to know where you are and the direction you want to go."

Annabel leaned closer, her interest growing as he explained the degrees marked between the cardinal points. His voice was firmer than usual this afternoon, and he spoke like a man who knew what he was talking about.

"Okay, say now you want to head south by southeast. Keep your needle on North and line yourself up with a landmark." He craned his neck, squinting at the compass and then on an angle to his left, and nodded. "That white pine there."

"Which pine?" Annabel asked. She could tell a pine from a fir but not one kind of pine from another. There were several pines in the yard in the general direction of his nod.

"That biggest one. The others are Norways. They got

longer needles, like bristles kind of, Norways. You see it?"

It was her turn to nod. Compared to the full, plumelike boughs of the one tree, those of the others did have a bristly, bottlebrush look.

"So I pick the white pine for my landmark. Then what?"

"Then you walk to it and line up another landmark farther on. It don't have to be a tree. It can be a rock, a bush, anything, but line it with your compass. And when you get there, look back to number one before you go on to number three, and look back again when you get to three. You want to make sure all your landmarks are lined up straight. That way you won't get to wandering in circles."

Like yesterday. Annabel struggled against a shudder. "You can bet I won't. I'm not getting that far off the road again."

Old Pa pressed the compass into her hand. "You take this." He shook his head slowly. "You don't know—Don't know her." His voice trailed off as if he had lost the thread of his thought.

"Who?" Annabel had to ask it, despite a warning tingle along her shoulder blades.

The old man shifted his weight restlessly, gazing beyond the porch at nothing as the swing swayed. "Ethel Gordon," he muttered, not talking to Annabel anymore, but speaking to himself. "Ethel—"

It wasn't the name Annabel had feared, but it was related,

somehow. Ethel Gordon would know what was meant by the message that Julia Craig was stirring.

Annabel stood up too abruptly to be anything but clumsy. "Well, I guess I'll go practice using this." Her laugh sounded phony even to her as she snapped the compass lid shut. "Thank you. I'll take good care of this."

Old Pa nodded absently while he rocked the swing, the fingers of one hand spread wide on one knee, his mind apparently adrift. He was like a radio, Annabel thought, powered by faulty batteries that operated for a little while after a rest and then faded out.

Ricky trailed behind her to the base of the white pine, and became an interested observer as she laid out a course using the compass. She was soon fascinated by the discovery that Old Pa's landmark system really worked.

Donna intercepted her on a northwest trek to the garage from a stand of poplars across the road. She had changed from her jump suit of the morning to white shirt and shorts divided by a broad red belt. "Hi. What you doing?"

Annabel made her explanation brief, feeling a trifle uncomfortable at being caught playing games. To her surprise, Donna said, "Neat! Can I try it?"

Annabel showed her what to do, and in a short time they were lining up landmarks together and giggling over their choices. They ended up in the hammock under the pines, sucking on cinnamon balls from a stock in Donna's shirt pocket, while Annabel gave serious thought to sharing with her the tale of the other Annabel.

"Been having fun, kiddies?" Todd asked from behind them. He gave the edge of the hammock an upward heave that all but dumped them on the ground.

"Cut it out, Todd," Donna shrieked, clutching at the tilting sides while Annabel stretched her legs to dig in her heels as a brace. "That's not funny."

"It is to me," Todd said with his high-pitched laugh. "Funnier than watching you two playing tree tag or whatever you were doing before."

"We weren't playing. We were finding our way with a compass," Donna informed him as he sauntered around in front of them.

"Oh, wow! And you got all the way from the garage to the hammock without getting lost? Let's see your compass."

"Old Pa gave it to Annabel. It's the one he used to have in the woods."

"I said let's see it." Todd's hand shot out. "Give it here."

Annabel's fingers closed protectively about the brass case she was trying to slip quietly into her pocket. "It's just a compass. An old one."

"Don't go thinking it's yours because Old Pa gave it to you. A broken-down zombie like him, living off Grandma and Grandpa, he's got no business giving away anything."

"I should think he's got a right to give his own stuff to anyone he wants," Donna objected.

Todd gave her a pitying stare. "Well, think again. I say no."

"Let's see what Grandma says," Donna said, and bent to adjust her sandal. "Annabel, come on."

A dingy pink began to mottle Todd's pallid skin. "Since when did you get to be Clarabell's dear little buddy?" He jerked a thumb in the direction of Donna's middle. "If that's the 'super red belt' you bought this morning, it makes you look like a sawed-off barber pole."

Donna didn't look up from her sandal strap. "How come Michael's not with you?"

Todd raised a scornful shoulder. "He's monkeying with his dumb films. I got better things to do than sit around in a dark barn all afternoon. Maybe Grandpa wants to take off and go fishing."

"He's not here," Annabel said, in no way sorry to disappoint him. "He left right after lunch."

Todd wheeled on her as if she had issued a challenge. "Left for where?"

Annabel shrugged. "I don't know. I saw him drive off in the jeep, that's all."

"The jeep," he said derisively. "He never goes anywhere in the jeep that we can't go along. If he was taking the jeep, why didn't he tell us?"

Annabel pushed a strand of hair off her face. "Maybe this once he didn't want you." It seemed a likely possibility.

Todd's pink splotches were growing darker. "We know who he wouldn't want. You're the one that's got him teed off at everybody. Why'd you have to be here this summer to screw up everything?"

Annabel rose slowly to her feet, gathering to herself every inch of dignity she possessed. "I wouldn't have missed it for the world. I'm having such a fun time."

Todd glared up at her, his eyes unwinking marbles. "Just stay out of my way, Clarabell Cow. Or I'll blow you off the road." He coughed, and caught sight of Ricky peering around the tree that supported one end of the hammock. "The same goes for you, you mangy mutt. Get out of here."

Annabel's lunge was pure reflex as Todd snatched a fist-sized rock from the ground. "No! Don't you dare!"

She seized his arm in mid-swing. The rock spun off course, landing wide of the dog. But Ricky was already in flight to the barn, tail between his legs, as though he had cause to suppose more rocks would follow.

Todd uttered a yelp and twisted to free himself. Annabel prudently let go and stepped back, although she doubted he could break her grip if she truly wanted to hang on. His muscles were as soft as the layer of fat that overlaid them.

"No wonder that dog's scared of his shadow," she said defensively. "Does Uncle Axel know how you treat him?"

Todd was wheezing like a runner in poor condition. "You keep your nose—" The words were submerged in a sputter of coughs. "Nose out of my—"

The effort was lost to another strangling cough. Veins

in his neck and temples bulged in a face going rapidly blue with the struggle to breathe.

"What's the matter?" Annabel gasped at Donna, even though the answer was an easy guess.

"The asthma. He's not supposed to get so mad." Donna gazed at his contortions an instant longer. "I better get Grandma."

Todd choked out a sound that somehow impressed Annabel that he didn't want his grandmother, but Donna was off and running. Annabel stood awkwardly where she was, torn by a wish to run off, too, and a fear of what worse might happen if she left Todd alone.

He was clutching at himself here and there, at his various pockets, in what seemed an aimless frenzy. Then he had a tube or bottle in his hand and was pumping spray into his mouth, his face turned from her as if this were a very private operation. When he turned back, stuffing the sprayer into a hip pocket, he was breathing without strain.

"You okay?" Annabel asked, hardly able to believe it could all be over so fast.

"Don't you ever try hassling me again." He swiped the heel of his hand across his forehead, erasing sweat beads. "Just keep your nose out of my business, and anything else that don't concern you."

He added an explosive word under his newly restored breath as Aunt Lil and Donna raced out of the house.

"Todd," Aunt Lil began calling. "Todd, honey!"

"What do you want?" he demanded in the tone of one whose patience was being sorely tried.

"Thank goodness." Aunt Lil hurried to take his arm as if she expected him to collapse on the spot. "I didn't know if you had your inhaler. Your mother will be so upset. She was afraid those new shots wouldn't be protection enough."

"You're not going to call her!" He sounded genuinely appalled. "You'll have her up here on the next bus. For nothing. Look, I'm fine." He dragged his arm from her and squared himself, shoulders straight, legs apart, in a rather flabby version of an athlete's stance.

"Yes, but if you've had an attack— I promised to tell her." Aunt Lil was shaking her head unhappily. "The responsibility's all mine when she's not here."

"I didn't have a real attack." Todd's voice was an exasperated whine. "I'm okay. I'm fine. I was only pretending, just clowning around. How'd I know these turkeys couldn't take a joke?"

Aunt Lil frowned, not yet convinced. "An attack is nothing to joke about."

"Well, it was a joke. There wasn't any of it for real. If you don't believe me, ask her." Todd aimed his elbow at Annabel. "And if she says there was, she's a liar."

Annabel opened her mouth and closed it without saying anything. She didn't owe him any favors, but if he preferred choking to death to calling his mother . . .

Aunt Lil's whole attention was fixed on Todd. "I don't know. If you're sure— Why don't you come inside, anyway, and have a glass of milk?"

Todd sighed, but let himself be towed toward the house.

Donna fell in behind, and for lack of anything else to do, Annabel did, too.

Food, she reflected. That was Aunt Lil's solution to everything. Have a glass of milk, a cup of tea, a couple of brownies and forget your fears, your hurts, your questions.

Michael emerged from the barn. He shouted to them, waving something in his hand, but a shout from Todd drowned him out. "There's Grandpa!"

He broke from Aunt Lil, nearly knocking her down in his rush to meet the jeep as it headed for the garage. "Hey, Grandpa, where'd you go?"

Uncle Axel stopped at the garage ramp and checked through several items on the seat before he got out. Annabel's stomach curled in on itself at sight of the tennis shoe in his hand.

"Where were you?" Todd insisted. "How come you didn't tell us you were going?"

"I went to the Craig cottage," Uncle Axel said, raising his voice to benefit everyone in the yard. "And I did what should have been done long ago—locked the doors and boarded over the broken windows."

He held out the shoe. "Here, Annabel. I think this is yours. Only I didn't find it stuck in the door sill. It was on the bed in that spare room off the kitchen."

He said it so severely it was almost an accusation. Who could doubt now that her story was—put in the kindest terms—one great confusion?

He was waiting for her to take her shoe, but she had to muster all her will power to make herself touch it. She would rather have accepted a handful of maggots, although she couldn't say why.

"Now, I hope that puts an end to this ghost business for the rest of the summer," Uncle Axel concluded, gazing hard at each youngster in turn.

A movement, like a small shiver, made Annabel aware that Michael was next to her. Whatever he had been waving on the way from the barn had since disappeared. His hands were empty, but in his eyes before they shied away from hers was a look that struck her as both guilty and not a little scared.

7

Rain began pattering on the roof sometime during the night. It rained all the next day and night and all the day after that.

"I bet those boys are up to something out there in the barn," Donna grumbled at bedtime. "They think they're safe because nobody wants to check on them in the wet. I should have brought my swimsuit after all."

Annabel was already comfortably settled against piled-up pillows with a book on dog training she had found in the living room bookcase. "How come you didn't bring a suit?" she asked, mildly surprised. "I thought there were all kinds of lakes around here, and public beaches."

"There are. There's even a neat little lake on this property, way back. Kind of muddy but fun." Donna pulled back her bedclothes and slid into bed. "But we can't go in when Todd's here because the water makes his asthma worse."

"Why can't you go in without him? He goes off and

95

does his own thing without you anytime he feels like it."

"I know, but—"

Donna didn't have to finish the thought. Annabel knew, too. Todd's mission in life was to make other people's lives as miserable as possible, and he worked at it with a will.

Like last night. She had been startled out of sleep by the crying of a cat. Body rigid, heart pounding, she had stared into the darkness, every nerve taut to hear above the pelting of rain on the roof. Then she heard Todd cough near the foot of the stairs, and soon after, Aunt Lil murmuring to him, ushering him back to bed, fetching him cough syrup or something from the bathroom. The cat didn't cry again.

If that didn't prove who'd been mewing, she could hardly miss reading the truth in the sly glances Todd kept slanting at her all day today. She had said nothing, since it would only be her word against his, but that didn't change what she knew.

Her hand slid up under the pillow to touch the smooth, cool case of Old Pa's compass. She couldn't prove, either, that Todd had sneaked up here yesterday to rummage through her things or that the compass was what he had been searching for, but it would take a great deal to convince her otherwise.

"I'd take it as a favor if you did keep it," Aunt Lil had said when Annabel told her of the gift. "It's been a long time since Old Pa's shown so much interest in anything as he did in hunting that up for you. You're a sweet girl to be so patient with him."

If looks could kill, Todd's glare would have shriveled Annabel on the spot, but he had walked off without comment.

Then, yesterday evening when Annabel came upstairs, she was struck by the rumpled appearance of the bedroom.

A drawer or two not tightly shut, a sweater on the floor, the corner of the throw rug kicked up—these she might never have given a second thought. Neatness was not her strongest point. But when she tripped over the shoe Uncle Axel had returned to her, it was a different matter.

That shoe had no business being out in the open. She had purposely kicked it and its mate as far under the dresser as they would go, wanting never to see them again. Merely dangling the missing shoe between a thumb and finger to carry it upstairs made her skin crawl, and it went on crawling until she had scrubbed her hands twice with soap and a brush.

But there the shoe sat in plain view on the little rug. Half a pace behind it was the toe of the other one poking from under the dresser as if the two sneakers had been halted in mid-step.

Aunt Lil, supposing her dust mop might have routed them from their exile, wouldn't have just left them wherever they happened to land. Neither was it Donna's way to leave things scattered about. Who else then but Todd? And why else but to take or tamper with the compass he so resented her having?

"Todd's not too bad in some ways," Donna said without a lot of conviction. "He's got worse problems than asthma, my dad always says."

It didn't take much genius to figure that out, Annabel reflected. She squared the dog training book on her knees. "Maybe one of them's those fancy cowboy boots. He sure acts like they pinch."

Donna giggled, nestling herself under her covers. "It's a side effect of his medication, Aunt Myrna, his mom, says. He's maybe not growing as fast as he should. Boots help him look taller."

Annabel was in no mood to dredge up sympathy for Todd on any account. "I should have such a side effect."

Donna curled on her side, her head propped on a hand. "You shouldn't put yourself down like that. You'd look really nice if you didn't slouch so much. When you forget about being tall and stand up straight, you've got a lot going for you."

Annabel sent a skeptical glance along the length of her narrow contours under the green-sprigged blanket. "Sure, if you're into flagpoles." But she straightened her shoulders, aware they had hunched automatically as she spoke.

Donna made a face. "How about being a sawed-off barber pole?" She sighed. "The worst of it is, he's probably right. I'm too short for wide belts. They make me look mostly all middle."

"He was just being smart," Annabel objected. "That's a great-looking belt."

"It would be perfect on you. Kind of cut your height." Donna sat up, tossing the bedclothes aside. "Why don't I put it out for you so you can try it on tomorrow and see? If you like it, it's yours."

"Well—okay, thanks," Annabel said, more taken by the friendliness of the offer than by any faith in the cosmetic possibilities of the belt. "I'll try it."

She seldom wasted thought on what she wore beyond whether it was clean and in a reasonable state of repair. To expect her clothes to do more for her than provide a decent covering was like asking a coat of paint to transform a ladder into a marble staircase.

Donna was padding in and out of the shadows beyond the light from the two bedside lamps. "I've put it over here on your dresser." Then—"Ouch!"

She sat down abruptly on the floor, grasping one bare foot in both hands.

Annabel let her book fall shut. "What happened? Stub your toe on something?"

"On your sneaker. Only it feels more like it kicked me."

And in fact, Donna was cradling her ankle, not a toe.

The hairs prickled along Annabel's arms as she got out of bed. "There shouldn't be any sneaker there."

"I know there shouldn't." Donna gave her ankle a final rub before she stood up. "It seems to me I shoved that shoe back out of the way just a little while ago."

Annabel ignored the possible hint that her housekeeping habits left something to be desired. Her eyes were on the sneaker lying in front of the dresser.

It was not one of the blue-and-white pair she had worn today. It was a red-trimmed black one she'd meant never to wear again. It was the sneaker she had tripped over yesterday when it lay exactly where it was now, a good six inches from the dresser it was supposed to be under. And there was the toe of the other one, just poking into sight, both of them pointed toward her bed.

The prickling on her arms spread upward to the nape of her neck. "You don't mean it was this same sneaker you shoved back," she said. "It had to be a different one."

Donna shrugged. "Maybe. But it was a black one." She nudged the offending sneaker with her foot, then frowned. "No, it was this same one. I remember the scrape marks on the heel."

The marks were familiar to Annabel, too. They were fresh, raw scrapes etched in the rubber by something sharp—like the splinters of a broken doorsill.

"I didn't leave it there. But this is twice it's been out here," she said in a voice that wanted to whisper. "Three times, if you shoved it back, too. It doesn't seem to want to stay put."

She and Donna stared at each other in the half light the lamps created at this end of the big room.

Donna forced a giggle. "Well, we know it can't be walking out by itself. It must be the floor's warped under the dresser or something and stuff gets jiggled forward when we go by. Otherwise, it should have followed you home instead of waiting for Grandpa to bring it."

Annabel had to grin. Put that way, her qualms did sound stupid. Besides, there was still her Todd theory to account for at least one of the shoe appearances.

Yet what of Uncle Axel's claim that he had found the

shoe in the bedroom, an unexplained distance from the kitchen doorsill?

Perhaps Donna, too, harbored a small doubt, for she added, "Why don't you shut them in a drawer so they have to stay put?"

"That's a super idea."

Annabel dropped immediately to tug open the dresser's heavy bottom drawer. So far she had stored nothing of hers in it, partly because two-thirds of the space was already taken up by an extra blanket, and partly because the capacious upper drawers provided all the storage space she needed. Also, this bottom drawer tended to stick, and came open only under protest. It was the perfect place for the troublesome sneakers.

Except for one thing. Now she was going to have to handle them again, pick them up. Kicking them out of the way wouldn't work this time.

Gingerly, she reached for the farther one and tossed it in. Then, her fingers clumsy with repugnance, she made herself lift the scarred one and let it fall beside its mate.

But the creepy feeling wasn't there. If anything, her hand felt pleasantly warmed.

Donna knelt with her to help wrestle the unwilling drawer closed. By the time the job was done, a tide of drowsiness was flooding Annabel. All at once she was as sleepy as though someone had fed her another one of Old Pa's tranquilizers.

It was as much as she could do to straighten her pillows

and switch off her light when she climbed back into bed. She exchanged a yawning "Good night" with Donna and was asleep before the thought more than half-formed that she should raise her head for a last look at the drawer to be absolutely certain it was tight shut.

Swiftly though sleep came, however, it was no blanket of oblivion. Several times during the night she was roused by an impression of odd noises and stirrings in the room. Once she even fancied Donna must be opening that reluctant drawer. But each time when she came awake enough to focus on the sounds, there was nothing, and she slid easily back into sleep.

The voice at first was only another annoyance nibbling at the edge of her consciousness. Someone calling her. She moaned a complaint and tried to wrap herself tighter in her cocoon of sleep, but the calling persisted.

"Annie! Annie! A-a-an-nie!"

Not just someone. It was her mother calling.

Annabel rolled over and sat up. How could her mother be here? This wasn't the Fourth of July. And what was she doing down in the yard, calling up to Annabel's window? And why "Annie," when her mother never called her that?

Annabel didn't stop to puzzle. She was already seeking her slippers with her feet, cramming herself into her robe. Next she was hurrying down the stairs in the gloom of earliest light. It didn't strike her as strange that no one else seemed to have been wakened yet by her mother's arrival.

As she crossed the silent living room, she became aware of mewing. Not the wail of the lost cat in the woods, but glad little chirps of the sort Muffin used to greet her with.

Muffin! Her heart jumped, and she flung open the door to the porch.

There stood her mother, Muffin in her arms. Muffin, who was not dead, but had merely strayed and now was found and brought back to her.

Annabel ran forward, arms outstretched as the gold-and-white cat leaped to meet her, uttering mews of delight.

But it wasn't Muffin. In the instant Annabel stooped to gather it up, it became a gray cat—a fluffy silver-gray cat with a white M on its face.

And that wasn't her mother waiting for her in the gray-mist shadows. It was an older woman, taller and heavier, her face framed in waves of carefully puffed white hair.

No matter. The cat was purring rapturously in Annabel's arms as if it belonged there. And she wanted desperately for it to belong, to be hers, a creature to love again and be loved by.

The woman smiled and nodded—a grandmother's smile promising cookies. She beckoned Annabel to follow her.

Annabel followed, understanding that in this way the cat could become hers.

They crossed the wet lawn under dripping trees without

speaking. Annabel bent her cheek to the cat's silky head, noting little else until gravel crunched under her feet.

She was on the drive. But not Uncle Axel's. His drive was paved with smooth blacktop.

The woman glimmered ahead of her, gliding on toward a mist-veiled shed. A garage, perhaps. A barn?

Annabel hesitated. Where was she? Somehow, she had traveled too far in just a few steps.

"Annie," the woman invited in a voice light as a whisper. Light as a current of air stirring. As the sigh of an old house settling. The shed doors, folded open, were clearly visible behind her—and through her.

"No," Annabel gasped. She couldn't find breath to scream. "No."

She tried to back away, but her feet were rooted.

The woman's smile widened, showing all her teeth. Hungry teeth. A gleaming death's head grin. "Annie."

Annabel's left foot began to slide forward. She couldn't stop it. The other foot shuffled past the first. One step. Another. A third. Her feet were carrying her slowly closer to the horror waiting for her.

She stared down at her feet—and at the sneakers on them. Sneakers that in her haste she had mistaken for slippers. Black sneakers that had not stayed safely shut away in the drawer where she and Donna had put them.

The cat evaporated into mist, wailing, as Annabel flung herself on the gravel, tearing at the shoes. She wrenched them off and hurled them from her.

"Annie!" Skeleton arms clad in shreds of rotting fabric reached out for her, lengthening and clawing.

Annabel scrambled to escape. Bony fingers bit into her shoulder. Others snatched at her robe. Grinning jaws, enormous, expanding, opened above her to take her in.

"Annabel! *An-na-bel!* Look at me. Can't you see me? *Annabel!*"

The whisper swirled around her like mist. She seemed to be in two places at once, struggling for breath.

There were other voices. Donna's: "Michael, don't. She's walking in her sleep. You're not supposed to wake sleepwalkers. You could hurt them."

"Bull." A third voice, rude, nasal, all too familiar. A stinging slap landed between Annabel's shoulders. "Come off it, Clarabell. What are you trying to pull?"

The ground shifted subtly under Annabel's bare feet. Wet gravel became cool linoleum. She blinked in the brighter-than-daylight brilliance of the fluorescent light overhead. The puffy moon of Todd's face was staring up at her. Michael and Donna were ranged beside him, wide-eyed, watchful, wondering. And they were all of them in Aunt Lil's kitchen.

"Where—" Annabel gazed around the room, not quite believing the grisly old woman could have retreated altogether.

"Right on, Clarabell, play it to the hilt." Todd switched to a beseeching falsetto. "Where am I? What happened?"

"Hush. Not so loud or you'll have Grandma and

Grandpa down here," Donna warned. "It's only five o'clock."

Michael hitched at the waistband of his undershorts, which, along with an undershirt, were all he was wearing. "Were you really asleep? Your eyes were open."

"I was outside," Annabel said uncertainly. "There was a woman—She called me to come out, and we went across the yard—" She clenched her hands on the edge of the counter behind her as a wave of trembling swept her.

"You were sleepwalking," Donna said. "You were dreaming. I could tell when you got up, so I got up, too." She combed her fingers through her tumbled hair. "I knew because Michael used to sleepwalk, too."

"When I was little and we'd just moved," Michael said defensively. "I wasn't tonight. Ricky woke me up howling, and then I got up to see why Todd was banging around. I saw the light on down here, and I came down."

"It wasn't me banging around. It was them." Todd pointed a half-eaten doughnut at the two girls. Without his cowboy boots and swathed in a wine-colored bathrobe fastened at his middle by a tasseled cord, he looked more squat and pudgy than ever. "Thumping and stamping up there like a herd of buffalo. I was about to come up there and drop it on you dumb turkeys."

Annabel pulled a chair out from the table. She had to sit down until her legs stopped shaking. Too much was pelting at her too fast. Could it be that she was the only one this night who hadn't been awake?

An open carton of milk stood on the table, three more

doughnuts beside it, but she saw no sign of a drinking glass. Probably Todd had been guzzling straight from the carton. The pig.

Somehow, that observation served to steady her a bit. Could it all have been only a nightmare? She would like to believe that, even though she could still almost feel the rain mist on her skin and the jab of gravel under her feet.

She pushed her hair back from her temples. It was damp, quite damp. But that could be from perspiration. There was nothing remarkable about waking in a cold sweat after a bad dream.

She groped in the pocket of her robe for a tissue to dab the moisture from her forehead.

"I heard somebody shuffling and bumping, too," Donna was saying, "but it wasn't us. You sure you didn't sneak upstairs anyway? If I'd waked up enough to turn on the light—" She broke off on a note of alarm. "Hey, Annabel, you all right?"

Annabel sat transfixed by what had slipped out of her pocket with the tissue.

It was a photograph, a black-and-white snapshot of a woman who stood resting her hand on the shoulder of a young girl with a large, pale cat in her arms. The woman was stout, white-haired, smiling possessively—

"That's her," Annabel breathed. Her mouth was so dry she could hardly shape the words. "She was outside on the porch. She was real—But then she was—Horrible!"

Donna leaned across the table to see. "Who is she? That

girl—that's not you, is it? When did you ever wear your hair short and curly like that?''

"That's not me," Annabel said fiercely. She pushed the picture from her as if by rejecting it she could change the fact that the girl caressing the cat did indeed have her face. "I don't know who she is. I don't know who either one of them is."

"Obviously that's not you, Clarabell," Todd said, returning to his doughnuts after a glance at the photo. "That one would have to stand on tiptoe to see in the upstairs windows. Besides which, the picture has to be over forty years old. It's one of the prints Michael made from those old negatives he swiped from the Craig cottage."

"And you guys doctored it up with Annabel's face because of the cat, then left it where she'd find it to make her feel creepy." Donna glared from him to her brother, fists planted on her hips. "Very funny, Michael. Really hilarious what you accomplished."

Annabel's heart began to slow its crazy racing. One of Todd's stupid jokes. Of course. A picture glimpsed perhaps too drowsily for her to remember but clearly enough for her strung-out nerves to weave its elements into a grotesque nightmare that actually lifted her from bed onto her feet.

"We didn't doctor it," Michael said indignantly. "That's just what's so weird about it." He turned to his cousin. "But you said you wouldn't show it. You promised."

"I said I wouldn't show Grandpa." Todd tilted the milk carton to his mouth and downed two noisy swallows. "Not that he couldn't find them himself, the way you've got them laying all over the place out in the barn. And I didn't show it to Clarabell. If she's got it, she picked it up herself."

"It was in my pocket," Annabel said. "I don't know how it got there."

But she was chilled by a memory of fleshless fingers clawing at her robe. At her pocket?

And the barn—Did that have folding doors anywhere? An apron of gravel? Suddenly she knew no power on earth could persuade her to go upstairs right now and check to see if those black sneakers still lay snug and dry at the bottom of the drawer.

"Don't forget, I heard those footsteps in our room," Donna said. She was accusing Todd, but the image of black sneakers that moved on their own stuck in Annabel's mind.

Todd's grin neither confessed nor denied. "You're getting as flaky as her?"

Annabel barely heard him. Something else was quivering at the edge of her mind, like a page about to be turned. Over forty years ago . . . She dreaded to turn that page, but even more to leave it unturned.

Slowly she took up the picture again. When she raised her eyes, Old Pa, in robe and slippers, was in the kitchen doorway. It was almost as if she had expected he would be there.

She stood up, holding the picture out to him. "Can you tell me who this is?"

Old Pa peered briefly at the photograph and nodded. "The old one, that's Julia Craig."

Todd expelled a derisive hiss, but Annabel made a flattening gesture with her hand that silenced him.

"The other one, the girl, who is she?" As if somewhere deep down she didn't already know.

Old Pa studied the picture more intently. "That's Julia's girl that she raised. Niece, she was. Named out of a book. Named—" He pushed his glasses higher on his nose, squinting as if the answer might be written on the photo. "Annie, they called her. Annie Craig. The one that run off with Walter Peterson."

8

"You're a Craig!" Todd drew back a step, his nose wrinkling like someone who has just discovered crawling things in his oatmeal.

Annabel stared past him at Old Pa, too stunned herself to take offense. She and Julia Craig were blood relatives? It wasn't by chance then, or mere whim that she had been singled out for Julia Craig's attentions? There must be a tie between them that, like a radar beam, would betray every dart and dodge Annabel made to escape.

"This girl is Annabel's grandma?" Donna asked. She held the picture now, examining it.

"Julia Craig only raised her. She wasn't her child," Annabel said in a last-ditch attempt to deny the connection. "My grandmother was an orphan."

"An orphan? Yes, from the time she was a little thing," Old Pa said musingly, as if the doors to his memory were gradually widening. "Typhoid or some such took off Julia's brother and his wife, seems like. I know Julia did a fair piece of traveling to fetch her."

"You could almost be twins," Donna marveled, raising her eyes to appraise Annabel. "The way your eyebrows curve, and the shape of your mouth, and the same long chin and straight nose—"

Curiosity overcame Annabel's dismay. She had been too unsettled by her first glance at the girl in the picture to note any details. "Let's see. I've never had a picture of my grandmother."

Her thumb slid to cover the older face as she took the photograph. It would be a long time, if ever, before she could glimpse that too-benign smile again without seeing it broaden to a skull's naked grin.

The girl's face was partly in profile, bent above the cat in her arms. Annabel had the uncanny sensation of staring into a mirror at a self that was and was not hers. Unlike the grab-bag effect of uncoordinated features she was used to confronting in the glass, there was a pleasing harmony to the pictured face, framed in its soft pageboy bob, as if the parts had been designed to go together.

The other Annabel—Annie—had been molded on a smaller scale, perhaps. It was difficult to tell her height from the picture, which showed her only from the waist up, but Annabel doubted her grandmother had lived with the dread of one day finding herself over six feet tall.

"She's not much older here than you, either," Donna observed, still comparing.

Annabel nodded. "She could be seventeen at the most. They eloped as soon as she turned eighteen, Aunt Lil told me."

Might plans to escape that hand on her shoulder have been simmering in the back of Annie's mind even as the camera shutter had clicked? Her expression gave no clue. She smiled down at the cat as if for that moment she was involved with nothing else.

Annabel knew well enough how that was. Hadn't Muffin's purr against her cheek often spun her a private world that was wholly invulnerable for a little space?

"They say Julia burned everything the girl left behind." Old Pa tore off a piece of paper toweling and began polishing his glasses. "Never spoke the girl's name again and wouldn't never let it be spoken. Just went straight through the house and got rid of every reminder."

Michael checked a yawn midway. "Hey, I bet that was her room—the girl's—we saw at the cottage. That empty room next to the kitchen."

"Julia was one that had to own things, and what she owned she didn't share. It had to be all hers or she didn't want any." Old Pa breathed on his lenses and rubbed harder.

Todd expelled a gusty laugh. "Even Craigs can't stand Craigs."

"It's Peterson she blamed for everything. Him and his." Old Pa settled his glasses carefully over his ears. "The last thing, she was about to take him to court over her claim that he was cutting timber with a long-handled axe—harvesting trees from her side of the property line."

"And then she disappeared forever." Todd raised

clasped hands above his head in the champion's salute. "Let's hear it for Great-grandpa!"

"Hush! Not so much noise." Donna pointed a warning finger toward the ceiling.

Old Pa folded himself onto Aunt Lil's step stool. "Peterson, he gave as good as he got. He was stubborn as they come, and he had a temper you didn't want to fool with." He shook his head, remembering. "I was there the day she lit into him in the post office for poisoning her cat. He blew up and told her where she could go and take her cat and her timber and her girl with her—told her so loud half the town heard." He paused to clear his throat. "That's the last day anybody ever seen her."

Annabel thrust the picture back in the pocket of her robe to keep from stealing another look at Julia Craig. "Was that before or after my grandmother died?"

She was beginning to understand why her grandmother had gambled on finding a better life somewhere else, and why her grandfather was not fond of visiting his old home.

Old Pa scratched his jaw. "As I recall it, they was still beating the woods for Julia the day of the girl's funeral. Must be Julia was gone first. It made quite a stir, the two things coming so close together like they did."

"Think of that," Todd said, pretending innocent wonder. "Could it be Clarabell's grandpa got his bellyful of Craigs the same time Great-grandpa did, and they each scragged them one."

Annabel's hand was in motion before she was aware

114

of where it was going. It flattened against Todd's greasy mouth with a smack that resounded in the kitchen.

His expression changed from disbelief to outrage, his color from paste to purpling red. His mouth opened, shut, and opened, but the only sound was a rasping wheeze as he strained for breath. He shook a fist at her helplessly, his other hand rising to claw at his throat.

For a minute, no one else moved or spoke.

Then Donna gave Michael a push. "Go find his inhaler. Upstairs, in his room, probably."

Michael sprinted out the door a split second before Uncle Axel, still buttoning his shirt, strode in. "What's all this racket? What are you kids up to at this hour?"

Aunt Lil crowded past him. "Todd! Oh, my goodness!"

Todd was bent double by now, his hands gripping a chair back in his struggle to drag air into his lungs.

Michael returned with the inhaler, and launched into a garbled account of sleepwalking, howling dogs, and how he'd printed up those pictures before Grandpa had pronounced the Craig cottage and its contents off limits. Donna was already pouring out her tale of fumblings in the night, nightmares, and practical jokes that weren't funny.

Aunt Lil clucked and cooed over Todd. Uncle Axel paced here and there, asking questions and frowning at the answers.

Annabel withdrew to the farther side of the refrigerator. There she stood looking on as if she were viewing a television show. She felt empty, and miles removed from the turmoil around her.

Todd's gasps became sputters of accusation against her. She watched the rosy swelling on his upper lip grow more obvious as the rest of his color faded to normal, and the effort to defend herself didn't seem worth the bother.

"Did you hear me, Annabel?"

She woke to the fact that Uncle Axel was in front of her, his hand out.

"I asked if you have that picture. I want to see it."

She yielded it up with a flicker of misgiving. "It's the only picture I've ever had of my grandmother."

He was rigid, staring at it.

Aunt Lil deserted Todd to crane over Uncle Axel's shoulder. "Julia Craig and Annie, sure enough. I didn't really believe it. Why, I never realized—" She glanced from the photograph to Annabel and back, her voice trailing off.

Uncle Axel muttered something short and harsh. His fist closed on the photograph, crushing it.

"No, don't!" Annabel grabbed for his sleeve in a useless attempt to save the picture.

He stepped out of her reach and tore the oblong of paper in half, and tore the fragments across twice more.

"I'm sorry."

He flung the scraps into the garbage pail under the sink. "But I'm not going to have that old business be raked up again. Just forget it. Michael, if you have any more of these printed, I want them, too. And the negatives."

Todd blew his nose loudly. "They're out in the barn. He's got a whole bunch of stuff in a big plastic envelope hid behind his bench."

Michael turned a bewildered glare on him. "That's my business. You said if I showed you, you'd never tell. You promised."

"I want to see them," Uncle Axel repeated grimly. "Go get some clothes on, and then show me."

Head down, Michael slunk from the kitchen at a far different pace from his dash to fetch Todd's inhaler.

Todd lolled back in his chair and blew his nose again.

"Fink!" Donna said distinctly. She twitched her robe tighter about her so as not to brush him as she passed. "I'm going up and get dressed, too."

Annabel would have followed her, but Aunt Lil laid a hand on her arm to stop her. "It's nothing against your grandmother, honey. Maybe if she'd lived longer—But sometimes it's best not to have reminders lying around of a bad time that's over and done with."

Annabel said nothing. She couldn't trust herself to speak.

Aunt Lil patted her arm and drew her toward Todd. "Now, I want you two to apologize to each other and shake hands. You're family, and you'll be glad of it some day."

Old Pa's rusty quaver interrupted from his stool. "It's not done with. Never was. She's waiting there, watching her chance, and she means mischief. But you won't see it, won't listen till it's too late."

It was true. None of them did listen. None but Annabel. Only the tightened line of Uncle Axel's jaw as he swung to glower out the window hinted that he had even heard.

Aunt Lil tugged Annabel forward and seized Todd's

arm so briskly she actually jerked him. "Now, say you're sorry and shake hands on it," she commanded. "Both of you."

Todd's moist fingers touched Annabel's and curled away. "She's the one should be sorry."

"I am sorry," Annabel said.

More than that: she was furious. Ice cold but seething. In less than a week, she had been scolded, humiliated, terrified, treated like a mental case, and deliberately misled if not lied to outright—all because of a stupid secret that should have been her right to know from the start.

She shook off Aunt Lil's hand. "I'm sorry I ever came here. I'm sorry I ever heard of this family. I'm sorry my dad didn't change our name to Smith and let the Petersons go jump."

She was backing toward the stairs, but she fired one more shot from the door. "At least the Craigs never murdered anybody!"

Uncle Axel pivoted from the window as if he'd been yanked by a string. "No Peterson has ever committed murder, either. Understand that. And don't forget it!"

His eyes, chill blue behind his spectacles, stabbed at her across the room, but she was beyond flinching. She raised her head higher. He was, after all, not quite as tall as she by half an inch.

"Why should I believe that? You don't. You're the one who's scared purple it isn't true."

A stifled snicker drew her attention to Todd. He was

sitting erect, grinning widely in anticipation of the disaster she was calling on herself.

"And you," she pointed at him. "So sorry you've got asthma. What would you do with no asthma to save you every time you chicken out?"

It was a low blow. So low that it felt inspired.

"Mischief!" she heard Old Pa repeating as she fled into the hall and up the stairs.

There were other voices in the upstairs hall. The door to Michael's room was open, and Donna, still in robe and slippers, stood just inside, her back to the hall.

"—so dumb," she was saying. "Plain, stupid, dumb. You know he'll rat. He always does. But you go right on telling him everything you know. You never learn."

Michael's retort was gruff from what might have been withheld tears. "And you have to put on such a big act always. Like you're so cool. Like nobody in the world knows anything but you."

Neither of them saw Annabel, and she didn't linger. Donna and Michael fighting? She'd never heard them quarrel before. And both of them were now at odds with group leader Todd. Could it be that Julia Craig was reaching out to touch them all?

Mischief . . . Mischief . . . The warning creaked from the steps as she ran up the remaining stairs. And by mischief, Old Pa didn't mean kiddie pranks like sneaking cookies; he meant it in the old-time sense of doing willful harm.

Annabel dropped onto her rumpled bed and stared at

her clenched hands. Was it possible she had just slapped Todd and insulted Uncle Axel and defied Aunt Lil? Surely someone would be coming after her soon to call her to account.

Well, let them. A punch of her fist sent her pillow skidding across the bed. What could they do worse than send her home where she wanted to be? Let her mother start being a parent again instead of a middle-aged schoolgirl indulging a crush.

No!

The objection broke so sharply into her thoughts that she turned, half-convinced that someone must have spoken it aloud. The room, its shadows banished by daylight, was empty of anyone but her. Maybe she really was beginning to lose her mind.

Without intending to, she let her eyes stray to the drawer she and Donna had struggled last night to close. They had done a sloppy job of it, she saw.

At one end, it was jammed in tightly on an upward slant. At the other, it tilted outward, leaving a gap wide enough for a hand to slip through. Or a shoe?

Her heart began an uneven beat, but she made herself walk over, kneel down, and reach inside. The black sneakers were there, exactly as they were supposed to be. Their coolness was clammy to her fingers, but she couldn't swear they were actually damp. No more could she swear that the sandy grit trapped in the rubber ridges of the soles had not been there last night.

And if she could swear it was, what of it? There would be some logical explanation that almost fit, as there was for everything else. She could march up to Uncle Axel with the ghost cat in her arms, misty and transparent, and he would somehow prove it was no ghost at all—and immediately proceed to kill it.

She sprang up, her angry grief at the loss of the photograph boiling over afresh. What other treasures that would now have meaning for her might there be in the Craig cottage? By rights they should be hers as Julia Craig's only living descendant. The cottage, too. What made Uncle Axel think he could lock and nail her out if—

If what? She pressed her hands on the dresser top, dizzied by the crazy path her mind was taking. Revisit that cottage? Wild horses couldn't drag her there if it contained all the wealth of the Indies, whatever that might be. It was as if, for a moment, another will than hers had been in possession of her thoughts.

She picked up her hairbrush and launched an attack on the snarls in her hair. The brush snagged on a tangle and twisted in her hand. Her impatient tug to free it brought tears to her eyes. It also flipped a lock of hair across her forehead, giving the effect of bangs.

When her vision cleared, her lean, too-long face had vanished from the mirror. The face that stared wonderingly out at her, nicely contoured and proportioned, was Annie Craig's.

Annabel was slow to understand, but when she did, a

121

vengeful delight filled her. To destroy a black-and-white photograph was one thing. Dealing with an image in living color would be quite another.

"What are you doing?" Donna asked from behind her without much interest.

Annabel resumed her brushing. "I'm thinking of cutting my hair."

"Hey, super." Donna's enthusiasm perked up a trifle. "Only have a professional do it. I know a neat shop in town where they don't charge too much."

"Okay, why not? I've got some mad money my mother gave me." Mad was the right word, too, Annabel reflected, and the result would be worth the expense. "Anybody in the bathroom, or can I go clean up?"

The delicate aura of after-bath lotion and scented shampoo that trailed Donna through the room testified that she'd already had her turn.

"Nobody," she said, hanging up her robe. "Grandpa just hauled Michael off to the barn. Todd's gone back to bed, and Grandma's still in the kitchen."

She unfolded a melon-colored top, considered it, and laid it aside in favor of a navy blue before she added, "Grandpa and Grandma had a big fight a few minutes ago. I heard them through the bathroom register."

"What about?"

"Old Pa, mostly, I guess. Like what to do with him, and what he says and like that." Donna returned the navy blue to the drawer and distractedly took up the melon again. "I don't remember that they ever had a fight before."

122

Annabel fished her slippers from under the bed and put them on. Mischief . . . Mischief . . .

The compass lay on the bed, its hiding place exposed by the pillow she had knocked aside. She tucked it in her pocket lest Todd recuperate and start prowling sooner than expected. Besides, the weight of the brass case was rather like an anchor to reality.

Until she woke to what was running in her mind: that a little more practice with it and she need have no fear of getting lost on a return visit to the cottage.

9

It was afternoon before Annabel trusted herself to venture out of doors.

She had ample excuse for staying inside had anyone questioned her. The return of the sun after two days of rain turned the morning into a steam bath laced with new-born mosquitoes that clung to the screens in visible clouds, whining hungrily.

But nobody did question her. Neither did anyone speak again of the events of the early morning—not to scold or to lecture or to speculate. The fact was, nobody was speaking to anyone of anything that wasn't absolutely necessary.

Aunt Lil made a stab at morale raising when the troops gathered glumly for lunch.

"I think what this group needs is a change of scene. We've been cooped up in one place too long. What do you say to a picnic at the lake tomorrow if it's a nice day?"

"We'll be eaten alive," Donna said without looking up from her plate.

"There's enough OFF in the cabinet to coat an army. Besides, there's usually a breeze at the beach that keeps the bugs away. It should be nice."

Michael's gaze traveled briefly past his peanut butter sandwich to a point in space just short of his cousin Todd. "What fun's a beach if you can't go in the water?"

"You like to go fishing," Aunt Lil countered. "I'll call Fuller's and have him save us a boat for tomorrow."

Todd's grunt was derisive. "One boat for all of us?"

Aunt Lil abandoned the discussion and turned to urging Old Pa to eat a piece of bread and butter with his chicken noodle soup.

The atmosphere wasn't brightened any by Uncle Axel's terse comment that Ricky was missing. Probably chased off after some female he got wind of and wouldn't be back for days, but it wouldn't hurt to keep an eye peeled for him.

No one left the kitchen in the company of anyone else.

Annabel, liberal daubs of mosquito repellent on her face and hands, the compass in her pocket, let herself unobtrusively out the back door. The compass was hardly an essential item for a tour of the back yard, nor did she imagine it had any magic properties that would keep her safe; but there was comfort in being able to touch the brass case now and again. Perhaps that was because Old Pa, in his befuddled way, was the one person who seemed to care what was happening to her.

There were two outbuildings behind the house besides the barn. One, whatever its use in former days, was now a garden shed. Hoes, rakes, spades, and coils of garden hose hung on wall pegs. Bags of fertilizer, grass seed, weed killer and the like sat on the floor, and clay pots lined the shelves.

The other shed housed a large garden cart, an array of axes and saws, and a shoulder-high stack of wood cut into fireplace lengths.

She circled each building in turn and stepped briefly inside. Anyone seeing her might suppose she was looking for Ricky on the chance he had returned.

Of course, she already knew that neither shed stood at the end of a gravel drive or had folding doors that opened into sinister blackness, but she needed to see once more that it was so.

The barn had doors at each end. She stood a moment at the foot of the dirt-and-stone ramp that sloped to the upper level where two big rust-red doors could be slid apart wide enough for a hay wagon to pass through. But sliding doors did not fold. Not even on a misty night could they give the impression that they folded. Nor could the hard-packed, weed-studded earth under her feet be mistaken for gravel.

The barn's other door was the one that opened by halves, top or bottom.

And that was that. No folding doors. No gravel paths. No shed anywhere that remotely resembled the one in her nightmare.

Why wasn't that a relief? Why couldn't she shake the feeling that the nightmare shed did exist? That even by daylight it yawned, waiting, somewhere.

Stop it! Think of something else, she commanded herself.

Ricky's broken chain lay across the concrete doorsill. She picked it up.

What a frenzy he must have been in to snap it in two like this. She hoped his lady love appreciated such a tribute. Odd that his howls had waked Michael, but she hadn't heard a thing.

Nothing but the cat's purr and that seductive voice calling her name.

Without wanting to, she glanced toward the woods. In the sunshine the leaves of oak, maple, birch, evergreens, and ferns gleamed a dozen different shades of green. Sunlight dappled the undergrowth, making it look far less dense than she remembered.

Something pulled at her to come, explore. Maybe Ricky's interests had got sidetracked in the woods, and she really could find him.

"You're too late. Forget it."

She flinched back onto the doorsill with a sense of having just escaped stepping off a ledge into thin air.

"Too late for what?" she demanded more roughly than she intended as she focused on Michael, scuffing across the yard from the house. "What do you mean?"

"If you're thinking you'll find more of those old pictures out here," he said, "they're all gone, prints, negatives, everything. Grandpa burned them up."

Annabel hoped the fumes from that fire had brought about Uncle Axel's poor appetite at lunch, but she managed not to say it. Michael's dull tone and slumped shoulders suggested he was feeling bad enough without help from her.

"What about the pictures you took that day at the cottage? Are they gone, too?" Silly to think they might not be. Uncle Axel was nothing if not thorough.

Michael shrugged. "I threw those away myself. The film was no good."

"Didn't they show anything?" She was unaccountably disappointed.

"They came out like overexposed with streaks of light across them. Just the first couple of shots were any good, the ones I took outdoors."

She dropped the dog chain and smoothed her hand over the pocket where the solid curve of the compass bulged gently. "How do you mean, streaks of light? What were they like?"

"Just streaks of light. White spots." His voice shrilled a little as he repeated. "It was a bad film. Defective, that's all. Nothing else."

"Okay. Okay." She found it hard not to be a trifle shrill herself. "I didn't say it wasn't, did I?"

He gave her a wary glance from under his brows, then slapped at a mosquito on his shoulder. "Anyhow, Old Pa wants you to come in. He's got company."

"Company? Old Pa?"

That was nearly as fantastic as wondering if something

other than faulty film had spoiled the cottage pictures. Old Pa lived alone on an isolated planet, like the sole survivor of a vanished race, despite all of Aunt Lil's fussing over him. Or maybe because of it.

"A couple of ladies," Michael said. "I don't know who."

It didn't matter. She was glad for a chance to oblige the old man. He didn't ask many favors.

She heard voices and light laughter from the living room as soon as she entered the kitchen. Perhaps she should make a quick detour upstairs to comb her hair, maybe put on a fresh shirt, and otherwise tidy up. Donna would.

But the stairs were blocked. Todd was seated on a step midway up, within earshot but out of sight of the living room.

"That's right, Clarabell. Keep going," he jeered as she swerved from the stairway. "The boogie man might get you if you stop."

She jerked her thumb toward the candy bar in his hand. "I'd be more scared of getting chomped to death by those perpetual-motion jaws. You never quit, do you?"

"You better believe it." His fingers went to his lip, touching it as if he could still feel the bruise there. "I owe you one, Clarabell. A biggie. And don't think I'll forget it, Clarabell Craig."

"Oh, grow up," Annabel said for lack of anything more appropriate. She wasn't exactly proud of having hit him, but that was altogether different from being sorry he got hit. "What are you going to do this time? More cat imitations in the middle of the night? Or will you paw through all my stuff again when I'm not there? That was really crude."

"You can't prove any of that."

"Surely you're not scared that I can, are you?" she asked, and left him coughing on a bite of candy bar he swallowed too fast.

Donna was standing by the fireplace in the living room. Annabel glimpsed her through the door and remembered to comb her fingers through her hair and fluff it up. It was more difficult to remember not to slouch herself smaller on the brink of being presented to strangers.

Aunt Lil spied her and called in a bright, company voice, "Annabel! There you are. Come in and meet the Gordons."

A woman in a green top and plaid cutoffs turned from admiring the African violets blooming on the windowsill. "Hello, Annabel," she said, holding out a hand. "I'm Sue Gordon. Mr. Schulty—" she nodded at Old Pa seated on the couch—"and I used to be neighbors when he lived in town. He grew the most delicious tomatoes I've ever tasted, and always buckets more than he wanted for himself, bless him."

"You're the milkman," Annabel said as recognition dawned. "I mean, person. Or—" She stopped, feeling stupid.

Aunt Lil rescued her. "She also teaches history and math at the high school and writes a column every week for the paper. This is her grandmother."

Annabel had already noted the elderly lady in a flowered pink dress who shared the couch with Old Pa.

"Mrs. Gordon," Aunt Lil said, raising her voice slightly and waving Annabel closer, "this is Axel's nephew's girl. This is Annabel."

"You don't have to tell me who this is." The old lady bent forward, surveying Annabel out of smiling gray eyes as alert as a girl's. She offered a wrinkled hand. "You're Annie Craig's—what would it be—granddaughter?"

And this had to be Ethel Gordon, the doctor's widow and Old Pa's canny schoolmate of long ago. Annabel was a little embarrassed to find she had only partly believed there still was such a person. Carefully she returned the surprisingly steady clasp of the worn fingers, and as carefully phrased her reply.

"Yes, she was my grandmother, but I never knew her, and my grandpa never told me much."

Mrs. Gordon clucked her tongue. "That sounds like Walter Peterson. A quiet boy always. He took it hard, losing Annie, and I suppose seeing you grow up so much like her, he's reminded all over again. You even hold yourself like her: tall and trim as a popple tree, I told her once."

"Thank you," Annabel said, less for the compliment than for the revelation. Was it possible—probable—her grandfather's reserve was not an expression of disappointment in her but something quite the opposite? She felt as if she had been handed a very special gift.

Donna flashed her an I-told-you-so smile and joined the group at the couch. "That's what I think, too. Annabel could be a model if she wanted to, I bet."

131

Old Pa gave a nod and chuckled. "The house is full of beautiful women. And an old codger like me, too old to enjoy it."

"Grandma and I thought you might like to take a ride with us this afternoon, Mr. Schulty," Sue Gordon said. "We're just going to cruise back roads and appreciate summer."

"Oh, I don't know," Aunt Lil said quickly. "Pa gets tired so fast, and then he gets kind of turned around and upset. Confused."

"Don't you let them tell you you're too old to have a good time, Henry." Mrs. Gordon gave Old Pa a playful tap on the arm. "It's sitting still with nothing to think about that makes you tired. I'm not as spry as I once was, either, but I'm not about to let them put me on the shelf while I can still wiggle, and I'm a good six months older than you."

Aunt Lil was shaking her head. "Pa was pretty sick there for a while. It took a lot out of him."

"Well, I ain't sick now," Old Pa said with startling decision. "And I guess it won't kill me to be seen in public with a pair of good-looking women."

Sue Gordon laughed. "Good for you. You were the inspiration for this drive in the first place. Your mention of Julia Craig last week gave me the idea for doing a column or even a series on the abandoned houses in this area. Grandma's come up with a lot of intriguing memories, and we thought it would be interesting to have a look at some of the old places."

Aunt Lil coughed delicately as if trying to clear her throat. She must be starting to feel haunted by Julia Craig, too, Annabel thought. And surely she was giving silent thanks that Uncle Axel had driven off to town after lunch and wasn't here.

"You aren't thinking of going to the Craig cottage, I hope. The road in there's too overgrown for anything but a jeep, and Axel's got the place all locked up and boarded over."

"They've locked that place time and again," Old Pa said contemptuously. "That's never stopped any that wanted to get in bad enough. Or out."

"Now, Pa," Aunt Lil interposed. "If you're about to go for a long ride, maybe you'd better use the bathroom before you leave?"

A dusky red welled up past the old man's open collar and into his face. "I guess I still know enough to use the bathroom if I need to." But his resistance gave way to Aunt Lil's upward tug on his arm, and he got stiffly to his feet.

Annabel cringed to see him towed from the room like a poorly trained preschooler. Did Aunt Lil want to cut him down in front of his friends, or did she think he was too old to have any feelings?

Indignation spurred Annabel to pull a chair nearer to Mrs. Gordon and sit down. Without caring if Aunt Lil might overhear, she asked the forbidden question, "Do you think the Craig cottage is haunted?"

She thought at first that Mrs. Gordon hadn't heard her.

The old lady laced her fingers together in her lap and sat studying them.

"They never found her," she said just as Annabel was drawing breath to repeat the question. "She had it all set down and filed away with her will, Julia did, you know: exactly how she wanted her funeral to be—which hymns should be sung, what Scripture verses should be read, what dress she should be laid out in—all that. She was a great one to want things done her way. But then they never found her. I've wondered sometimes if she could have been buried like she wanted, if she'd have rested easier all these years."

Donna hitched herself onto the arm of Annabel's chair, her eyes wide. "Does that mean you do believe she haunts that cottage?"

"Yes," Mrs. Gordon said slowly, "I believe it. Something's there that shouldn't be." She unlaced her fingers and looked at the girls. "It's been a long time since I've heard any talk of the place, but there used to be such tales told—and some by the last people you'd ever expect to see a ghost, or admit it if they did. It seems that when there's young people near she's provoked the most and folks start hearing Annie's cat."

"Annie's cat?" Annabel repeated.

"Oh, yes, the ghost cat." Sue Gordon had dug a small notebook from her handbag and was flipping the pages. "Haven't you heard how it haunts the woods, calling for its lost mistress? The story is—" she consulted some jottings in the notebook— "Annie, for some reason, couldn't take her cat with her when she eloped. Her aunt guarded it after that as the one hold she had over Annie that might finally draw her back."

Mrs. Gordon's chuckle carried the breath of a sigh. "Annie did love that cat. Julia was so protective and watchful, it was about the only playmate the poor child had. I recall one time when the doctor and I stopped by when we were out for a drive, and there was Annie playing house under the lilacs, with her cat—hardly more than a kitten then— wrapped in a doll blanket like a baby and purring his silly head off."

Annabel's smile was one of recognition. She and Muffin had played let's-pretend games like that, too.

For the first time, though, her pleasure in the parallels between herself and her grandmother was edged by a shadow of unease, as if there were a danger of her own identity being nibbled away by too many likenesses. She was Annabel, complete, separate, individual. She was not— she would not be—Annie Craig come again.

Donna was slowly shaking her head. "Why would she do anything that would bring Annie back? Old Pa said she burned up all Annie's things and wouldn't even say her name. It would make more sense to think she was the one that poisoned the cat."

"Julia didn't bother much about making sense when she thought she'd been done an injury. I think that deep down she did want Annie back—Annie was all she had—but I don't doubt she would also have made her pay dearly," Mrs. Gordon said, shaking her head in turn. "She went

135

a little crazy, I think. The doctor suspected she'd had several small strokes during the year, but she paid no attention to his warning that she might have a serious one if she didn't try to take things calmer. She flew all to pieces at her cat's death." A pause and another head shake. "No, definitely Julia didn't poison it—if anyone did."

"Wait a minute. What do you mean, if anyone did?" Sue Gordon plopped herself on the end of the couch Old Pa had vacated. "I must have been in kindergarten the first time I heard that poison story, and now you're hinting it wasn't the dastardly deed we all grew up on? You've been holding out on me."

Annabel and Donna looked at each other and quickly looked away.

Could the "dastardly deed" have been recounted often without dragging in Oscar Peterson's name? Annabel tried to stifle a twinge of doubt that perhaps Uncle Axel did have some justice on his side, that forty years hadn't buried the old, ugly rumors so deep they couldn't surface again with only slight encouragement.

"I guess you never asked me," Mrs. Gordon said, laughing a little as Sue poised her pen above a notebook page. "Certainly poison makes a better story, but I've always wondered. There were so many cats that sickened and died that spring. Cat distemper, we called it. In those days there weren't the shots they have now to protect your cat and prevent such epidemics. I remember that one particularly because at the time Julia was crying poison and foul play, we'd just lost our dear old Danny and the last of her kittens."

She pursed her lips, watching the pen scribbling across the page, then added a shade more sharply, "Of course, Julia's losses were always greater than anyone else's."

"Maybe she didn't care if it was poisoned or what," Donna said indignantly. "I bet all she wanted was a chance to make trouble."

Sue Gordon's mouth drew tight like her grandmother's. "Well, she succeeded. Beyond anything she could have dreamed."

Mrs. Gordon shifted on the couch as if she were losing interest in the conversation. Her old voice sank to a note that was barely audible, but it retained its sharp edge. "You youngsters stay away from that haunted cottage. There's harm enough on this earth done to each other by the living without hunting for more from the dead."

Annabel turned, following the direction of her gaze.

A transformed Old Pa was being shepherded into the room by Aunt Lil. His soup-spotted shirt was replaced by a natty blue knit, his rumpled suntans by soft gray slacks. The lower part of his face glowed pink from recent use of a razor, and his sparse hair was brushed smooth. He looked as scrubbed and neat—and as unhappy—as a little boy dressed up for Sunday school.

"Ready to go?" Sue Gordon asked, getting to her feet.

Old Pa's face brightened a degree. "If you ladies think you can keep up with me."

"Now, he's got a bottle of pills in his shirt pocket, Sue, if he needs them," Aunt Lil began. "And you've got your handkerchief, haven't you, Pa? If he starts to feel queasy or get drowsy—"

She was still issuing instructions, admonitions, and advice through the car windows when Sue, her passengers comfortably bestowed in the back seat, started the engine and began to move down the driveway.

Annabel waved good-bye from the porch, although she wasn't sure any of them saw her. She slid her hand into her pocket and curled her fingers around the compass, thinking of Henry Schulty, who used to work in the woods and raise delicious tomatoes in his own garden before he became Old Pa. It kept her from thinking too hard just yet of anything else.

"I'm glad it's daylight and sunny," Donna said at her side as if she preferred to drop the subject for a while, too. "Were you serious about cutting your hair? I can call that beauty shop and get you an appointment. We could bike into town for it if we can't get a ride."

Half an hour later Annabel was on her way upstairs to check the funds in her wallet. She stopped in the upper hall to give the frowning photograph of Oscar Peterson a searching study. Could he actually have committed murder?

The Gordons, she realized, had given her no more answers to anything than she'd had before.

"Annabel?"

It was Michael, mounting the stairs warily to join her.

After a glance behind him and up and down the empty hall, he pushed a Spiderman comic book at her. "Here."

She took it and, puzzled, riffled the pages. They opened to where a black-and-white snapshot was wedged between them like a bookmark.

"It's off that bad film I told you about, but this one's not too messed up, and it's got you on it. You can have it."

He didn't wait for discussion or thanks, but retreated to the bathroom and shut the door.

Annabel went on upstairs to her room. She sat a long time on her bed, contemplating the picture.

At first look it was not too impressive—a shot of the big lilac tree near the Craig cottage. Plainly, she'd been included only by accident, a not-quite-in-focus figure at the far right. The cottage didn't show at all.

What did show was one of the light streaks Michael had complained of. It was a pale, rounded spot at the base of the tree, something like a thumb print in shape. Or rather—

Annabel shut her eyes and opened them to look more intently at the configuration of leaves and twigs surrounding it and of those dimly visible through it. The longer she stared, the more definite the outline became: a silvery, transparent, crouching cat.

A nnabel hid the picture under the newspaper lining of her top drawer. She didn't look at it again. She didn't have to. She could call it up in exact detail simply by closing her eyes.

Still, she slept soundly that night, untroubled by horrendous visions or by dreams of any kind that she could recall the next morning.

"If you kids haven't anything better to do," Aunt Lil suggested, "you might put in some time on your bikes hunting for Ricky. I suspect he's hanging out somewhere in the neighborhood, making a nuisance of himself."

"No thanks," Todd yawned. "I'm not biking in this weather. That dumb mutt's not worth getting worn out and sweaty for."

Nobody argued. Nobody urged him. Annabel, Donna, and Michael just left him sitting on the porch swing, staring somewhat incredulously after them as they wheeled out of the garage together and onto the road.

"He's going to be mad," Donna said, sounding more clinical than concerned. "He didn't think we'd go if he wouldn't."

Michael kept his eyes straight ahead. "We never did it before."

"I guess he'll live," Donna said, a shade grimly. "And so will we."

They didn't find Ricky, although they searched along a dozen branching roads and scouted a score of farmhouses and summer homes, peering into yards and calling him by name.

Todd was still sitting on the swing—or more likely, sitting there again—when they returned at last to flop onto the porch steps. They were as tired and hot as he had predicted but feeling good about themselves and deserving of the lemonade and ginger cookies Aunt Lil wheeled out to them on a serving cart.

"Perfect, Grandma," Michael sighed, downing a glass in two long gulps. "Thanks."

Todd reached for the cookies. "We're having strawberry ice cream in super-cones for the picnic. With walnut cake and pineapple punch, besides barbecue and hot dogs and baked beans and all the rest."

"What picnic?" Donna directed the question at her grandmother, not glancing at him. "That's not still on for today?"

Aunt Lil laughed, refilling Michael's glass from a fat plastic pitcher. "With a menu like that? No way. I'll need a day at least to put it together."

"It's day after tomorrow," Todd said. "All day."

Annabel shook the weight of her tumbled hair back from her face. "That's Friday. That's the day I'm getting my hair cut."

"At ten-thirty," Donna filled in. "We told you, Grandma. You said it was okay." She eyed Todd over her lemonade. "And you were right there. You heard us."

"Oh, yes, of course. Honey, it slipped my mind." Aunt Lil struck her head as if to clear it. "Well, we can have the picnic Saturday. No problem."

"No, we can't." Todd's boot soles slapped the porch floor. "Everybody's at the lake on Saturday. There won't be room to turn around. Besides, I called the boat place and the deal's all set up for Friday, nine o'clock."

Donna let out a squeal. "You did that on purpose. You knew we had other plans."

"Tough," Todd said with a shrug. "Where does it say the world stops just for you? Either you hang in or you get left behind."

Annabel gave him a narrow look over her shoulder. If this was his way of getting even, he was due for disappointment. Uncle Axel's chill nod at breakfast had sealed her resolve to have those bangs if she had to cut them with nail clippers in front of the bathroom mirror. That might be the best way to go, anyway, for she had never been inside a beauty parlor. What if she did or said something stupid there that would turn Donna off just as they were starting to be friends?

Aunt Lil waved the lemonade pitcher for silence.

"There's still no big problem. Grandpa can take you boys fishing in the morning, and I'll drive you girls into town and pick up some last-minute things like the ice cream. We can all meet at the picnic tables at noon. A whole day at the park is probably too much for Old Pa, anyhow."

They bickered among themselves a while longer after she took the emptied cookie plate inside, but in effect, the matter was settled—nobody the winner, nobody the loser this round.

So, shortly after ten-thirty Friday morning, Annabel found herself recklessly answering, "Right," to a woman in a pink jump suit who asked, "You want a general trim and shaping, too, along with the bangs?"

The woman, who was Sheri according to the name embroidered across her pocket, swathed her in a plastic cape and proceeded to wield comb and scissors like a chef with fork and carving knife. Nothing further was expected of Annabel, obviously, except to hold steady and watch the showers of cut hair slide down the cape to collect in a dark drift on the floor.

"You've got beautiful hair. It just falls into place," Sheri said as if she understood this was a moment for reassurance.

In almost no time, she spun the chair to face the broad mirror. "How's that? Pretty much what you had in mind?"

Annabel's first reaction was disappointment followed by dismay. The bangs were feathered wisps and tendrils on her forehead, not the heavy fringe of the photograph. And the rest of her hair was layered in soft waves, a sleek update of Annie's fluffed pageboy. She wasn't seeing Annabel anymore—not the Annabel who had seated herself here twenty minutes ago—but she wasn't seeing a portrait of her grandmother brought to life, either.

Then Sheri swiveled the chair a fraction more. Like magic, the strange face in the glass, caught slightly in profile, became the face Uncle Axel had thought to be rid of by tearing up a picture.

"Neat," Donna said, circling for a view from every side as Annabel paid at the front desk. "It really suits you. You know, you look like—" She frowned, cocking her head to one side. "Like somebody I've seen. On TV, maybe?"

Annabel waited, wondering with a tingle of excitement if she would make the connection.

But Donna gave up the puzzle. "I'll think of it later. There's Grandma outside. Come on."

To Donna, after all, Annie Craig was only a flat image in black-and-white that she had no special reason to remember distinctly. It would be different for Uncle Axel.

"Hurry up and pile in, girls," Aunt Lil said through the open car window. "I want to get this ice cream home and into the picnic cooler before it melts." She gave Annabel a distracted glance of appraisal. "How nice and cool you look. This is the day for it, too. I can't believe we're this warm in June."

"Too hot. Too quiet," Old Pa said as Annabel slid onto the back seat beside him. "Weather's breeding. She's going to be a big one when she breaks."

He was fussing with the dark glasses snapped to his

spectacles, and didn't notice Annabel's appearance at all. She hadn't actually expected him to. He'd grown vaguer and testy these past several days.

Aunt Lil said his ride with the Gordons had overtaxed him. He'd come back from that ride, though, more talkative and alert than Annabel had ever seen him. In fact, he was so full of having stopped in to see Mrs. Gordon's apartment—its convenience, its comfort, its built-in safety features that let her live independently yet able to summon help quickly if she needed it—that Aunt Lil had wearied of the subject.

"Why that poor old lady has to live alone when she's got so many children and grandchildren that could take her in, I don't know. There's enough of them so there wouldn't any one have to keep her more than a month or two at a stretch if they can't find it in their hearts to have her full time."

Old Pa had dropped the subject and drifted back to his room, where he'd stayed most of the time since.

Aunt Lil flipped on the turn signals, swinging the car into the left lane. "A good storm would be a blessing if it cleared the air. But not today, thank you. Although Timber Lake Park does have a big pavilion for shelter if we did get rained out."

"Timber Lake?" Why did that name ring off-key in Annabel's ears?

"It's the biggest lake near here," Donna supplied. "Besides the park, there's a resort and private cottages and woods and even an island."

Plus it wasn't any great distance from the farm, Annabel soon discovered. After a stop at the house to collect the picnic hamper and cooler, they were hardly on their way again when they turned off the road and halted in a pine-shaded parking area. Uncle Axel's jeep was among the handful of other cars already there. Beyond, dark-rimmed toward the horizon, the lake shone blue and wide and totally unfamiliar.

Old Pa rested on his cane, gazing up at the trees. "Jack-pine. All second-growth stuff," he dismissed them. "Come in after the good timber was logged out, the white pine and the Norway."

"Well, Pa," Aunt Lil said, handing the hamper to Donna, "you should know. You did your share of the logging."

Old Pa nodded. "Yes, ma'am. Bull bucker, that was me. Foreman of the crew." His chuckle was as brittle as the needles underfoot. "We skidded a lot of logs across Timber Lake ice. Let a lot of daylight into the swamp."

Timber Lake—Why did those words give Annabel the feeling that prickles of hair had worked down inside her shirt despite the protective plastic cape? It nagged at her as, carrying the cooler, she followed Donna along a path that led to picnic tables set back above the lakeshore. There was something about Timber Lake she ought to remember. Something she almost did—

"At last! Food!" Todd was sitting on a shady table, dangling his booted legs as if he'd been there for hours. "Where have you guys been? We're starving."

146

"Where's all the fish you were going to catch?" Donna countered. "Did you eat them?"

Michael emerged from the other side of the table. "We caught a whole mess of fish. Enough for supper. Want to—" He stopped, his blue eyes rounding at Annabel.

Donna laughed. "Doesn't she look different?"

"What's new about that? Different's the only way she can look." Todd lifted the hamper from Donna and set it next to him. Then he stared, too.

Annabel placed the cooler in the center of the table, ignoring him.

"Brother!" he said half under his breath. His tone was almost admiring. "You're really asking for it, aren't you? You really are."

There was recognition in Michael's face, too, but no glee accompanying it. "Here comes Grandpa. Tell him I'm helping Grandma bring the grill." And he was off at a run.

Annabel turned, knuckles on hips, to watch Uncle Axel climb the stone steps from the beach. She wasn't as eager to confront him as she had thought she would be, but she was braced to stand her ground.

He saw her. His face was partly hidden by sunglasses and the brim of a straw hat, but she could tell he saw her because he stopped smiling. She hadn't even noticed the smile until it was gone.

His face thinned, as if the skin had tightened, and his lips pressed themselves together. He looked like a person who had stepped on a sharp stone and was trying not to show it—pained more than angry.

Annabel kept her head high, but she wished all at once that she had worn a hat, too. The day was unbearably warm, almost suffocating. And was it her imagination, or had the lake lost a degree of its shimmer in the past few moments? The pale sky gone slightly dingy?

Aunt Lil and Old Pa arrived at the table, providing a welcome interruption with the bustle of getting him seated comfortably where he could see the lake.

"It's going to be a while before we eat, Pa," Aunt Lil told him. "Axel has to get the grill set up and the charcoal started. Maybe you'd like a little ride in the boat while you're waiting."

Old Pa shook his head. "Too old and too stiff for boats," he said wearily.

Todd put on an earnest face as he opened a can of grape juice he'd extracted from the cooler. "We were kind of planning to take the girls over to see the old logging camp on the island, Grandma."

And his heart would be utterly broken if he had to forego this pleasure, Annabel thought, even if it were for the greater joy of entertaining Old Pa.

Donna was suspicious, too. "Who's supposed to do the rowing?"

Todd's smile was pitying. "We've got an outboard. Of course, anyone can row that wants to. Except her." He waved the juice can toward Annabel. "She probably hasn't got the strength now she's got her hair cut."

Uncle Axel's set mouth relaxed in a half-grin, and Annabel felt herself turning red.

"Try me," she challenged unwisely.

A gleam lit Todd's white-lashed eyes. "Okay. How about across the lake and back—in time to eat."

"No, now hold it just a minute." Uncle Axel was grim again. "Across the lake is out. I don't want you kids over on that side. You hear me?"

Todd shrugged. "No sweat. There's no way she's going to make it even to the island. You watch."

"The island's plenty far enough. You keep in sight," Uncle Axel said firmly, but not because he was concerned that other terms would be too harsh for Annabel, she suspected.

She wondered if privately he wouldn't be as tickled as Todd to see her get her comeuppance. Too late now to confess that she'd been in a boat only once, and that so long ago she hardly remembered anything beyond standing between her father's knees to touch the oars while he worked them.

Todd herded her and Donna and Michael down the beach to a green rowboat tied alongside a low pier. At least she did know to take the middle seat and face the stern. Mastering the rest couldn't be that difficult.

It would have been easier without Todd sitting on the stern seat, observing every clumsy move she made, but she managed to get the boat underway after a few experimental bumps and splashes. Rowing was actually rather fun once she began to get the hang of it.

Or it would have been had the day been cooler. No breath of air stirred the water's surface or fanned the beads of sweat that began to roll from under her new bangs. Her shirt was soon sticking to her back like wet Kleenex. But she was resolved neither to quit nor complain.

"What was that?" Michael asked unexpectedly. "Thunder?"

"How could you hear thunder out of a clear sky?" Todd asked. "What you hear is Clarabell panting through her big mouth." He stretched lazily. "Trying to get breath past the foot she stuck in it."

Donna stopped trailing her fingers in the water and straightened up. "I thought I heard thunder, too. Besides, this is dumb. Let's start up the motor and go back."

Todd flung an arm across the top of the motor as if to shield it from tampering. "Everything's dumb to you lately. Talk to her, your new buddy. Nobody's forcing her to keep rowing. She can throw in the towel any time."

Annabel glanced over her shoulder at the sky. It was clear, if by clear Todd meant cloudless, but the dingy tone she had noticed earlier was more of a dirty yellow now. It didn't look exactly wholesome.

But there was more to take stock of than sky. She hadn't realized how close they were to the island that was supposed to be her goal, or that when they pulled abreast of it they would have covered a good two-thirds of the distance across the lake.

Dense, dark woods marched along the forbidden far shore. No boat landing or summer cottage such as were sprinkled so liberally around the rest of the lake broke its long, sombre curve. Her impression was of uninviting dankness and gloom. She wasn't sorry Uncle Axel had put it off limits.

Suddenly she had no desire to row farther from the park. Donna was right. This was dumb. What could Todd do if she turned back right here except squall like the overgrown infant he was?

She dug the left oar into the water, straining to push the boat around.

The right oar twisted under her palm and bounced up as if it were on springs. Ice-cold water cascaded into the boat, drenching her and the seat opposite.

The squawk that broke from Todd was so like the yelp she'd been imagining from him, her own gasp became a giggle. And the giggle bubbled over into a laugh.

"You did that on purpose," he raged at her between swipes of his arm across his streaming face. "That was no accident. If I get sick—"

Annabel bent her head on her knees, too convulsed to defend herself. Dripping, fuming, and flapping, he put her irresistibly in mind of an angry Donald Duck. It didn't help any that Donna and Michael were laughing just as hard behind her.

"What was that about a towel?" Donna gurgled.

Annabel couldn't resist: "Nobody forced you to sit in that seat."

Todd was on his feet and made a show of starting for them.

"Hey, quit stamping." An edge of alarm thinned Michael's mirth. "You're tipping the boat."

The clunk of wood against wood, the splash, and Todd's, "Nice going, Clarabell. Now look what you've done" slashed away what merriment remained.

Annabel didn't know quite how it had happened, but an oar lay adrift in the water. Donna snatched at it, but it was already riding out of reach on the ripples set up by the rocking boat.

Annabel seized the other oar in both hands and leaned her weight into closing the gap, but she succeeded only in shipping more water. The floating oar, caught by an unseen current, angled away from the boat on a quickening course of its own.

"Lay off, you klutz," Todd shrilled at her. "You've got to be the world's prize disaster area."

He turned to the motor and brought it sputtering to life.

Even at that, the oar continued to elude them, bobbing tantalizingly close one moment, picking up speed and forging well ahead the next. It led them close to the island and past it and into the waters beyond, teasing them farther and farther.

What if it were luring them on deliberately?

Annabel squelched that idea as soon as it slid into her mind. She had problems enough without inventing more.

At last Michael, stretched nearly full length over the bow, uttered a grunt of triumph and hauled the fugitive oar aboard.

"Maybe we should check for a secret propulsion device," he commented, grinning. "Who ever saw a plain old oar take off like that? That's really weird."

"It wouldn't have happened if we'd turned back when I said," Donna reminded them. "Now we're right where Grandpa told us not to go."

Annabel was all too aware of that. They were in easy hailing distance of the brooding old trees of the far shore, had anyone been there to hail. A hard-to-define staleness weighted the air as if it had hung here, undisturbed, for a long time. That was only her imagination overworking again, of course, but she did not like this place.

She jumped as Todd cut the motor. "What are you doing? Aren't you going to start back?"

"Maybe we're out of gas, and you'll have to walk back," Todd said amiably. "Now we're here, don't you want to go ashore and have a look?"

Michael squirmed uncomfortably on his seat. "Come on, Todd. Grandpa's going to be mad."

"Grandma should have the hamburgers cooking by now," Donna added in a transparent attempt at psychology. "They'll be done before we get there."

Todd smiled at them while the boat glided steadily shoreward under its own momentum. "Think he'll be so mad if we catch his dog for him? Maybe I just saw that dumb mutt poke his head out of the bushes up there."

"Ricky?" Annabel turned to squint more intently into the dimness under the pines. White pines, her mind registered. An ancient stand that had somehow escaped the

153

axes of Old Pa and his crew. Virgin timber on Timber Lake. Timber Lake—

"I don't see him. Where?" Donna cupped her hands to her mouth. "Here, Ricky. Here, Rick. Come on, boy."

"There! There he is!" Todd pointed. "No, now he ducked back again. You saw him, didn't you, Michael?"

Michael shook his head. "No."

"Sure you did. You must have. By that big rock?"

"I don't know," Michael said doubtfully. "Maybe. It might have been something—"

"You call him, Annabel," Donna said. "He'll probably come for you."

"That mutt's not coming sloshing out to a boat for anybody," said Todd. "He hates water. If you want him, you're going to have to go ashore and grab him. Two of you, at least."

Annabel and Donna looked at each other and at the shrinking strip of water between them and the pebble-strewn beach. The boat nosed into the shallows and came to a stop with a small shudder.

"Come on, come on," Todd urged. "Get going if you want him, so we can get back to the picnic. There he is, still by that rock."

Donna scrambled to the tip of the bow and jumped. She landed stumbling but dry-shod.

Annabel was less lucky, perhaps because she was less willing. Those woods were too silent, too still. She shrank from raising her voice in that unnatural hush. She didn't want to push through those motionless branches.

Her reluctant jump plunged her ankle-deep in chilly water, and jarred further considerations from her mind for the moment. Aided by Todd's hoot of laughter, she hustled over slippery rocks and up the sloping beach to join Donna.

Donna, a few yards into the woods, stood frowning. "There's a house up there a little ways. Stand over here and you can just see it. I thought these woods went on forever, but they don't."

Annabel's heart squeezed to a standstill. She knew where they were. She knew even before the roar of the outboard starting up spun her and Donna around.

"Todd Peterson! Michael!" Donna screamed at the retreating boat. "Don't you dare—"

Todd waved at them. "Sorry, girls. I was right the first time. You'll have to walk back."

"No! Wait!" But somehow there were branches everywhere, holding Annabel away from the beach.

"Say hello to Auntie Julia for me," Todd called, pointing. "Tell her too bad we couldn't stop, but—"

His voice vanished in a clap of thunder that shook the earth. The sky split apart, and darkness spilled across it from horizon to horizon. Yet the lake in that same instant gleamed silver under a blue-white glare of lightning.

And in that instant, Annabel saw the wind. Saw it before its howl blasted her eardrums. Before its impact bowled her backward off her feet.

She saw it race toward her over the lake, driving the flat water into ridges, creaming the surface into foam, and rising under the green boat in a monster billow that curled to fling boat and boys high up on Julia Craig's shore.

 11

Darkness. Howling, battering darkness.

Annabel struggled up on her knees and crouched against the base of a tree. The trunk was more than the reach of both her arms in circumference, but the wind whipping around it tore at her almost as if she had no shelter at all. She could feel the branches straining overhead, sending tremors down to the ancient roots, tugging to dislodge them.

Lightning again. A blue-white sheet of it like the beam of a gigantic searchlight.

It picked out Donna, hunched under the tree, too. Her mouth was open in a scream that was lost in the uproar of thunder and wind. Annabel realized her own mouth was open, and that her throat ached from sounds that couldn't be heard.

She and Donna clutched each other's hands as the darkness shut down again. Something grazed Annabel's cheek—a pebble, a twig—she didn't know what. The air was full of flying debris.

Another flare of lightning. Donna pulled at her and pointed. The boys were coming at a stumbling run over the stones of the shore. Behind them the lake was hurling itself in wild, foaming surges at their heels.

This time when the dark returned, it was not quite so thick. Or else Annabel's eyes were becoming adjusted. She could still make out the running shapes and the shadow that was Donna, frantically waving them on.

"Over here," Annabel yelled, as if yelling were any use. "Hurry." It didn't seem to matter anymore that the boys—Todd, anyway—had meant to leave her and Donna stranded here just minutes ago.

Michael was first to gain the tree. Todd pushed in after him, shoving to claim the place nearest the protecting trunk.

A blast of thunder pressed the air from Annabel's lungs. Lightning flowed down the length of a tall pine, tracing every branch and needle in a momentary glow.

Donna's voice shrilled above a lull in the wind: "—house up there—just a little way—"

"No!" Annabel grabbed at her. Sheltering under a tree might be risky, but it had to be better than tempting whatever lay waiting in that terrible cottage.

The wind rose sharply as if to silence her. Added to it was a new sound—a kind of gasp and shudder among the branches overhead. She shrank back against Todd as a limb the size of a young tree crashed down only inches from them. The ground shivered with the impact.

"Peel!" Todd yelled, and pushed her aside.

He plunged off into the woods, angling away from the fallen limb and the now-charred pine. So did Michael and Donna. Then Annabel was running, too.

Any direction but toward that cottage, she told herself fiercely. Hadn't she glimpsed a big rock thrusting out from the trees farther down the shore? A rock big enough to offer some shelter from the wind?

Rain pelted her like spray from a hose. She ducked her head and dodged from tree to tree, trying to stay parallel to the shoreline or where she thought the shoreline was, trying to allow for the rushes of wind that staggered her off course. Daggers of lightning startled her into unintended detours. Wildly raking branches barred her way here, sprang up to let her pass there.

She realized slowly that she was on a path—a track of pale gravel laid down through the trees. Gravel . . . The feel of it under her sandals woke a horrid memory.

She turned to escape to the left, but the way was blocked by a tangle of deadwood. To the right, a row of close-set trunks hemmed her like palisades. She ran on, searching each side for a break.

Without warning, the trees gave way in front of her. She was in the open. The gravel path, more distinct now, unwound ahead of her across a pine-ringed clearing to where the cottage sat waiting.

She fought in vain to turn back. The wind swooped in behind her and lifted her onward as if she were late for an appointment.

Michael, Donna, and Todd came spilling out of the

woods, following the gravel path, too. They all tumbled onto the weathered front stoop together. The top of a birch tree sailed over the yard after them to lodge like a barricade against the bottom step.

"We can't get in," Annabel yelled in one final effort to fend off the inevitable. "It's locked. Nailed shut."

She knew a flicker of hope as Todd wrenched at the door without success.

"Let's go round back." She motioned the way. "Behind the house." They would be cut off from the wind there and much of the pounding rain. "We don't have to go in."

"Look out, will you?" Todd was wielding a heavy stick.

With a single, surprisingly expert swing, he shattered the glass in the door. Another two or three blows knocked out most of the jagged pieces that remained. He reached inside, undid the bolt, and turned the knob.

Before he could let go, the door blew inward, dragging him along. The same gust caught Annabel. She clutched at the doorframe to stop herself, but Donna and Michael slammed into her from behind and she lost her hold. It was as if the house inhaled them in a huge gulp.

"Shut it!" Todd was shouting from across the room beyond reach of the blowing rain. "Shut the door!"

Billowing draperies snapped like whips. The old rocker by the window started a furious rocking. A magazine that had lain untouched for years sped flapping toward Todd like a vengeful bird.

"The door!" Todd bellowed. "Shut the door!"

Michael hurled his weight against it and forced it shut. At once the uproar of the storm was throttled down to what wind and rain continued to drive in through the broken pane.

But the energy rampaging through Julia Craig's front room was not that quick to subside.

The rocking chair rocked on, inching farther out from its corner with each forward lurch. The magazine fluttered at Todd's feet as if it would rise again. And Donna struggled to loosen a loop of tattered drape that circled her neck like a noose.

"Look out!"

Michael's warning sent Annabel leaping sidewise just as a picture in a massive frame left the wall to pitch onto the spot where she had been standing.

Michael, dodging it, too, slipped on the wet floor and went down hard amid the shards of glass from the door. When he scrambled up, it was onto one knee. His hands were clasped over the other, blood welling between his fingers.

"Nice going, Julia baby." Todd kicked the magazine toward the rocker. "Scrag a Peterson or blow your image."

"D-don't!" Annabel's heart was jammed so far up in her throat she could barely scrape the word past it.

Todd produced his whinnying laugh. "Don't what? Bug an old cow that's so long gone you can't even smell her?"

"Todd, shut up." Donna swept a nervous glance about

the storm-darkened room as she sank to a crouch beside Michael. "Just shut up. Please." Her rain-wet neck bore a mark where the dusty drape had wrapped it.

"You think old lady Craig's going to pop out of the woodwork, too?" Todd's tone was withering. "Maybe along with the Tooth Fairy or one of Santa's elves? We can have her busted for trespassing if she does. Grandpa owns this place, not her." He rapped his knuckles against the wall. "Hear that, Julia baby? Mess with us and we'll blow the whistle on you."

The house rattled from top to bottom as if his knock had shaken it loose from its foundations. Thunder rolled and faded. The wind hushed for an instant.

And a new sound grew in the room.

"Listen." Michael looked up sharply from the Kleenex Donna had given him to press against his knee. "The clock's ticking. It wasn't doing that before."

Annabel was already fumbling behind her for the doorknob. "We have to get out of here." But her fingers couldn't seem to close on anything.

A tingle crawled along her nerves, raising the hairs on the back of her neck as if she'd touched a low-voltage wire.

Something struck against the house. Or was it something upstairs, moving? The attic door stood open.

Donna uttered a strangled gasp. She was pointing to the rocking chair.

A glowing ball of blueish light hovered on the seat. As Annabel stared, it bounced to the chair arm. And bounced again to the cat basket on the windowsill.

"Keep away!" Todd shrilled as the thing bounced to the floor and started gliding forward over the moth-eaten carpet.

Annabel abandoned hope of escaping through the front door before the thing reached it. "Out the back way," she croaked in what was meant to be a shout. "Run!"

Donna dragged Michael up by his arm. He came two steps and the injured knee buckled under him. Annabel sprang to catch him by the other arm.

Perhaps that was Todd's intent, too. Perhaps he didn't simply barrel into them in a blind rush to save himself. But the four of them were knocked sprawling, Donna and Michael in one direction, Todd and Annabel in the other.

Annabel regained her feet only to be sent staggering backward by another shove from Todd.

"Out of the way."

The ball had bobbed in between them and the other two. Todd sidestepped left, then right, trying to edge past it, but it headed off each attempt. At the same time, it continued to advance on him with a menacing electric crackle.

Annabel, behind him, was forced to back step by step as he did. He gave her no opening to try a break of her own.

A doorway rose up around her. Her heel bumped against a stair riser—the attic stairs.

She fought to stand firm as Todd crowded backward into her. Nothing could drive her up those stairs.

Todd's elbow jabbed her fiercely in the stomach. "Move, you stupid cow!"

Annabel's wince cost her her stand. Sparks snapped from the oncoming ball, and Todd slammed the door shut. Annabel was trapped with him in the narrow, dark stairwell.

Anger kindled beneath her terror. The impulse to fling the door open and him through it to clear a path for her own escape was almost overwhelming.

She was actually groping past him to find the door when the need to grope retreated. The darkness was thinning. Thinning fast. Yielding to a murky light that seemed to be growing out of nowhere.

It was light enough now to see her question chalked on Todd's face: That thing on the other side of the door, could it strain itself through wood to get to this side?

They turned and fled together up the cramped stairs.

But the light was stronger up here. A milky kind of radiance filled the attic, yet somehow failed to banish any of the shadows. The brightest spot was the old mirror against the chimney.

Annabel chilled at sight of her reflection there. It had to be hers: those were her faded denim shorts and her orange top on the mirrored figure. But her new hairstyle— Wind and rain had beaten it to where she was no longer an Annie Craig look-alike. Looking from the oval of the tarnished gilt frame was a living portrait of Annie Craig.

The milky light surrounding the reflection began to swirl like the flecks in a snowstorm paperweight. A shifting blur at first, a thickening mist, a discernible form . . . Then Julia Craig stood beside her in the mirror, smiling as she had in the photograph Uncle Axel had destroyed. Her arm lay across Annabel's shoulders in that same possessive pose, but without quite touching her—yet.

Annabel stared, spellbound. The noise of the storm on the roof was deafening. Through it, though, the whisper swelled, vibrant, inviting: "*Annie*—"

What if she accepted that invitation? One step, two—

Another sound tugged at her mind. Choking. Someone gasping for air.

She couldn't tear her eyes from the mirror, but now she was looking harder into its depths. Where was Todd? He should be reflected there, too. He hadn't been more than half a pace behind her.

Julia Craig's image wavered briefly, and Todd appeared, but insubstantial and gray like a double exposure. He was contorted, dimly but desperately, in a battle for breath.

Julia Craig's form steadied, sharpened, and blotted him out. *Blotting him out.*

"No!" Annabel was startled by the ring of her own voice. Not that she owed Todd anything, but he was a human being at least.

"*Annie*—" An element of command slid into the whisper.

Annabel's breathing was nearly as ragged as Todd's, but her capacity for cowering had been stretched to its limits. "No!"

She dropped to a crouch that ducked her reflection from under Julia Craig's tightening embrace. "Not Annie. Annabel. Annie's dead."

A shimmer like a ripple on water passed over the mirror.

Annabel braced for she didn't know what. Her fingers brushed and closed on something—a book on the floor. Perhaps the very one she had pulled from the bookshelves her first time here.

"Annie's dead," she repeated as the clear-cut image of Julia Craig began to shred along the edges into milling flecks of light again. "You'll never get her back. There isn't any Annie anymore."

As she spoke, the light beyond the mirror swirled in toward it, breaking into particles and swarming like infuriated bees over Annabel's reflection. She heard a moan mounting to a shriek. The floor shuddered beneath her. The roof opened above her. She sprang up, hurling the book full force at the glass, and was borne down into darkness by a crushing rush of air.

Stillness. Utter stillness.

That was what she was first aware of when her senses began bit by bit to return. No storm. No voices. No eerie whisperings.

A heaviness weighed on her shoulders. Another rested across the backs of her legs. She had an impression that a lot of time had gone by—hours, perhaps, or days. Or a century.

Little arrows of pain shot up her neck when she tried to turn her head. She opened her eyes to a fretwork of daylight slanting through what appeared to be a low canopy of pine boughs. Yet she was lying on the boards of the attic floor.

She moved her head again, testing. It hurt, but she could do it, and move her arms and her legs as well.

Slowly, awkwardly, with frequent pauses to grit her teeth against a surprise pain, she squirmed herself free of the branches that held her captive.

She really was still in the attic. But the attic was a shambles.

The chimney was a pile of rubble. A portion of mild blue sky showed through a gap where part of the roof was gone. Beneath it, fragments of broken mirror glittered on the floor. One of the big bookcases lay flat on its face. The other leaned above it, most of its books tumbled from the shelves. The wardrobe that had so long presented its back to the world was tilted around to display a tier of sagging drawers.

And jammed diagonally across the space from the stairway to the chimney sprawled a giant white pine, its trunk thicker than the rafters it had splintered in its fall.

Annabel swallowed. Her body felt like one big bruise laced by smarting cuts and scratches, but nothing seemed seriously out of order. It would have been a different story had she been struck down by that main trunk instead of only the springy, lightweight upper branches.

Missed again, Julia, she thought shakily. Then she remembered Todd.

She found him by following the sound of labored breathing, a sound she'd been hearing all along without registering it. His eyes were open, staring up at her, when she pulled aside the branches that hid him, but there was no recognition in the stare. She wasn't sure he was actually conscious.

Better if he wasn't, she thought, when she saw how a split fork was closed like a vice on his ankle. She didn't have a prayer of forcing those stout branches apart enough to set him free.

That was hardly a prime concern, though, when he was as gray as the mirror had shown him and gasping for each breath as if he were drowning. What if he should die right here in front of her?

She started a frenzied sifting through pine needles and twigs, chunks of mortar and other litter on the floor. Hadn't he been gripping his inhaler in that glimpse of him in the mirror? It had to be near him somewhere.

It was—flattened and useless under a stone from the chimney.

She couldn't go for help. The only way down from the attic was the stairs, and the densest part of the tree filled the place where they ought to be.

Donna and Michael, what had become of them? She held her breath, listening for a movement downstairs. There was nothing. Only the same unnatural silence. As if everything in the world had stopped, been shut off.

"Donna? Michael?" she shouted.

The silence only pressed in tighter.

She shouted again, directing her voice down the stairwell as close as she could get to it. And again, out through the opening in the roof, until it was too much like the day she was lost in the woods and had shouted herself hoarse with no one to hear.

". . . for within an hour's time there grew up all round the park such a vast number of trees . . . neither man nor beast could pass through."

Except that on that day there had been someone who did hear her at last. Her hand slid into the pocket of her shorts where she had tucked Old Pa's compass this morning for safekeeping. Just the solid, smooth feel of it drew away some of her panic.

Maybe she couldn't get out of here by herself, but there was nothing that said she couldn't try. Nothing, provided it was beyond Julia Craig's powers to reassemble that mirror.

The crunch of mortar grit and slivers of glass set Annabel's teeth on edge as she began a slow turn in quest of anything she might use for an axe or a saw. Gravel underfoot and mist-shrouded folding doors—the vision shuddered through her mind.

Then, a quarter turn more, and the vision was real. She was standing where she had stood that night, looking in through those gaping doors.

It didn't matter that after the first jolt of recognition she could see them in the daylight for what they were: a broad bookcase knocked forward and propped at a tipsy angle by its own spilled books, an old wardrobe spun outward into the room and away from the wall it had faced. Daylight showed her, too, what had beckoned to her from the blackness beyond them that other time.

Even so, she could have mistaken it for a heap of discolored rags back under the eaves. Except for the pale skull mocking her from eyeless sockets with a fixed-forever grin.

 12

The persistent jab of pine twigs between her shoulder blades and the increasing discomfort of sharp-edged rubble beneath her brought Annabel to a slow awareness that she was sitting on the floor. She had no recollection of her knees giving way, and no idea how long she'd sat hunched where she was, arms hugging her bent legs.

She did know that never while she lived would she forget a detail of the scene in front of her—the grimy lamp, its wick burned to ash generations ago; the moldering carton that contained something like a rolled-up doll blanket; the open shoe box on its side with a string-tied packet of letters spilled from it. And huddled on the floor beside these things in the secret space the wardrobe and bookcase, standing nearly shoulder to shoulder, had kept hidden more than forty years, the bones of Julia Craig.

Annabel uncramped her arms cautiously, as if a sudden movement might yet call unwanted attention to her presence. Her eyes felt as if she hadn't blinked for an hour.

The skeleton grinned on mirthlessly, one arm extended toward the letters as though pointing.

Annabel inched forward to crouch where she could read the topmost envelope without disturbing anything. It was addressed in a pretty, slanting hand to "Miss Julia Craig, Oneida, Wis."

No great surprise in that. It was the postmark that gave her a small start: Chicago.

Then she saw the sheet of paper that lay behind the box. Thin trails of dust marked where it had once been creased to fit an envelope, but the few lines scrawled on it in a large, square script were still as legible as print:

April 18, 1939

Dear Miss Craig:

    Annie died at 3:57 this morning, forty-two hours after the birth of our son. She was hopeful to the end that you would reply to one of her letters someday, but time ran out. You will not be troubled by any further correspondence from me or mine.

Walter Peterson

Annabel's own grandfather reporting in grief and anger the loss of her young grandmother so many years ago. And that newborn baby was to become Annabel's father. She drew back, disturbed by a thought that her being here completed the circle, like the princess who, despite all precautions to save her from the wicked prophecy, climbed a tower and pricked her finger on the kingdom's only spindle.

Annabel rubbed her arm across her face. The tree, and Todd, and getting help, that's what she should keep her mind on.

Her heart gave a jump. Someone was calling. Uncle Axel, downstairs, shouting, "Todd? Todd?"

Annabel flung herself onto the thicket that barred the stairs. "Here! Up here!"

She heard the stair door open. "Annabel? Are you all right? Where's Todd?"

"He's here. I'm okay but he's hurt. His foot's caught, and—" She paused to set her teeth hard into her underlip. This was no time to start crying. "The inhaler's broken, and he needs it."

"Okay, okay," Uncle Axel said briskly. "We've got a CB radio with us. I'll put in a call for an ambulance. We've already got men and saws on the way."

"How did you know?" She didn't much care, now he was here taking charge. She just wanted him to talk to her and go on talking.

"We were out cruising the lake for you as soon as we could get a boat. We found Donna and Michael down on the shore. The boat owner's taking them back to their grandma." His voice began to retreat. "Now I'm going to radio for the ambulance."

"No, wait." Annabel flicked a glance behind her and

took the plunge. "Uncle Axel, there's a skeleton up here. Julia Craig, I think."

There followed such a profound silence, she wondered if he were gone. Or was he once more fighting to keep his temper in leash?

"Tell me about it," he said finally on a carefully neutral note.

She understood in that moment that the whole story was something she could probably never tell. Not even to gain a measure of distance between it and herself. She would have to live with it always locked away inside her like a genie in a bottle.

What she described to Uncle Axel was only what he would see for himself when he broke through to the attic.

"Yes, it does sound possible." He cleared his throat. "Well, a skeleton can't hurt you. Just stay calm and do what you can for Todd. We'll have you down from there as quick as we can."

She found an old cushion and slipped it under Todd's head to raise him a little. There wasn't much else she could do for him, except to sit by his side, telling herself skeletons can't hurt you.

Cars, two or three of them, were drawing up outside. Men were talking. Almost immediately the machine-gun chatter of a chain saw started up. Soon there was a beautiful, ear-splitting chorus of them at work, some outside, and at least one below her near the stairs.

The skull stared unwinking at Annabel, looking oddly like its teeth were clenched. Tremors passed over the pine branches like the ghost of a bygone wind. The huge tree stirred. Before Annabel's unbelieving eyes, it lifted, rolled, and settled itself heavily again.

Todd shrieked as the shift wrenched his trapped ankle. Dust and dirt rained down from overhead. A slab of roofing crashed in, torn from the ragged break overhead.

Annabel shrieked, too. "Stop! Stop!"

It was impossible that she and Todd could have been heard, but the saws sputtered to silence. There was shouting, arguing, swearing.

"You want somebody killed, you go ahead cutting like you're making firewood," a voice, familiar yet different, rose above the others. "I can tell you how to drop her where you want. You get on it here at this side—"

It was Old Pa out there, wide awake, firm, issuing orders like the "bull bucker" he used to be.

One by one, the saws resumed their snarling. Tremors shook the tree again, but it did no more turning.

Annabel thought she heard a siren, the ambulance, perhaps, but she couldn't be sure over the noise. Todd was moaning now between gasps, but it wasn't only for his sake she wanted to scream to the men to hurry. Shadows were gathering in the corners and creeping over the grin under the eaves. Having to look at it was troubling enough. To know it was there and not be able to see it would be immeasurably worse.

The top of the stairs began to reappear through the screening brush. Then the saw shut off, and a red-bearded man scrambled up past the remaining branches.

"Hi, there. Got room for company?"

He wasted no time coming to kneel beside Todd and administering an injection from a doctor's kit he carried. "Relax, son. This will clear your pipes for you."

A balding man clambered out of the stair hole after him. Together they strained the pinching fork apart and released Todd's foot.

"Not to worry. He's going to make it," the balding man told Uncle Axel, who was next to join the group. "I could wish this guy had gone a little lighter on the pie and cake, but I guess we can manage to get him out of here in one piece."

Neither he nor the red-beard had noticed the skeleton in the shadows yet, but Annabel saw Uncle Axel's eyes find it. "Tell me what to do to help," he said and, amazingly, put an arm around Annabel's shoulders. "Why don't you lead the way down?" He gave her a small squeeze. "It's just about all over but the shouting."

All over. How she hoped that was true as she picked her way down the trash-strewn stairs to a living room littered with sawed-off boughs, splintered lumber, and fallen plaster. Could it be quite over while anything of Julia Craig was still sheltered by these walls?

She turned at the open door, her gaze tracing the zigzag scorch marks on the carpet. Freak lightning. That's how that crackling ball of light would be written off. Maybe it was. She'd read of such phenomena herself.

And the frustrated fury that had gone berserk in the attic? A random accident of the storm, nothing more. That last roll of the tree, too, that could have brought the roof down on them. Another accident, of course, the mistake of unskilled loggers.

She made herself walk, not run, on out the door into the light of early evening. Pink-tinged clouds drifted above a lake that glinted like crinkled foil—a lake that never before had been visible from the cottage.

Julia Craig's treasured woods lay on the ground, uprooted and shattered almost to a tree. The mammoth pine that sloped from the cottage attic to a splintered stump a good twenty yards away was just a part of the ruin.

All over? Surely it had to be. Any force must have exhausted itself in dealing wanton ruin on such a scale.

Three men stood consulting by a smaller tree the pine had bowed in its fall. The white-haired man, grown taller somehow, his stooped shoulders squared nearly as straight as he must have carried himself forty years ago, was Old Pa. He saw Annabel, and gave her a jaunty wave that was half-salute, half-caution. "Stay back, girl. Keep a safe distance."

The warning shout came as she was raising her hand to wave in reply. There were a dozen explanations afterward of how and why, but none could change the fact that the great tree trunk slipped suddenly sidewise, and that only two of the three men were quick enough to get out of its way.

13

Annabel listened, dry-eyed, as the minister spoke the final words over Henry Schulty the following Tuesday. It was a quiet funeral, just the immediate family, Mrs. Gordon and Sue, and the two men who had been consulting with Old Pa when the tree slipped. These men had hardly known him before that, but he had won their respect. He would be pleased by that, Annabel thought.

"He wasn't ever happy at our place," Aunt Lil kept mourning when she wasn't reproaching herself for having let him go in the search boat with Uncle Axel. "It didn't matter what I did for him, he just wasn't happy. I'll never understand it."

But he had been happy that last hour of his life, Annabel knew. She had seen him with his dignity given back to him for a little while, and she doubted he would count the cost too great.

The bones of Julia Craig were quietly buried that same day under the headstone that had waited for her so long.

Ricky came home the next afternoon, thin and ravenously hungry for the dish of Dog Chow and table scraps Aunt Lil gave Annabel to feed him, but wagging his lopsided corkscrew tail as if he'd never been away.

Annabel sat on the back step in the dusk, alternately hugging and petting him until Uncle Axel called her inside to share in the phone call he was about to put through to her grandfather in Albuquerque.

"I want him to have the straight facts before some busybody sends him a wild piece out of the paper," he said severely, but he couldn't hide the grin—an actual grin—that spread across his face as he began to tell his news into the phone.

"Right. That's how all the evidence reads: She died alone, very likely the same day she got your letter telling of Annie's death. It could have been a heart attack or a stroke. She was a prime candidate for both, you may remember, and a little balmy, besides. That old tale that she'd burned up everything of Annie's was a lie. She had everything squirreled away in a kind of secret hiding place in the attic, stuffed into a wardrobe trunk she kept facing the eaves so nothing showed but its back—everything from stuffed toys to the high school yearbook. Also every letter of Annie's from Chicago after you two were married, all of them opened, presumably read. It looks like she'd gone upstairs to file yours there with them and just keeled over doing it—maybe from the shock or grief or plain cussedness, but in the last place anybody would think to hunt for her. "

The receiver was warm from his hand when he finally passed it to Annabel.

"You're all right, Annabel?" Her grandfather's voice came over the wire more agitated than pleased. "You're sure?"

"I'm fine. They checked me out at the hospital and sent me home. Todd's still there, mainly because of his asthma, but he has a broken ankle, too."

Stupid things to say. Why not add that Michael's cut knee had required three stitches? It wasn't likely her grandfather even knew who Todd and Michael were. But what was there to say to someone who wasn't much beyond a remote acquaintance himself?

"My mother's coming Saturday," she babbled on. "I told her I'm okay, but when she saw the storm pictures on TV, she made up her mind she should come." Moreover, her mother had been so full of anxious questions, she hadn't once mentioned Donald Kimball.

"I don't blame her. She must have thought you were off to a nice, safe, wholesome vacation when she sent you up there. If I'd known she was even contemplating such a move—"

Annabel pulled a chair closer and sat down. He wasn't talking about the storm. He couldn't be. He was saying he could have foretold the vacation wouldn't be safe or nice or wholesome.

"It was pretty scary, some parts of it," she admitted, testing.

"Yes, I can believe that," he said slowly, as if he might

179

be reviewing the possibilities. "Another thing I believe is it's been too long since I've seen you. That's got to be remedied before the summer's over. Maybe we can talk better then."

Annabel hung up feeling slightly stunned. By "talk better," did he mean she could tell him everything? Would she dare? The answers, she realized, were less important than the discovery that he genuinely cared what happened to her.

She should have dreamed pleasant dreams that night, but a vague impression of something left undone nagged at her through all of them. It was the same thing the next night.

Then, in the small hours of Saturday morning, it wasn't a dream anymore. She was lying wide awake in the dark, listening to a cat crying close by.

Just an ordinary cat, she told her jumping pulse, a coincidence, a serenading tom . . . But she knew what it was. And by daylight she knew what she was going to have to do.

She thought wistfully about waking Donna for the sake of company, but persuading her might prove a day-long job, supposing she could be persuaded at all.

Annabel scribbled a note in lipstick—Donna's—on a corner torn from the newspapers Aunt Lil used for drawer liners: "Back by breakfast. A." and tiptoed downstairs.

She had to go out by way of the kitchen. Todd, released from the hospital yesterday, was sleeping on the living room couch because the cast on his left leg made climbing stairs out of the question and he would have no part of being put in Old Pa's room. His mother, Lydia, was asleep in the living room, too, camping in a sleeping bag. She had hardly gone farther from his bedside than the bathroom since her arrival in near hysterics the day after the storm. She and Todd were flying home to Milwaukee this afternoon.

"And I bet he never even gets to try those crutches," Donna predicted. "She doesn't think they're safe. She doesn't think anything's safe unless it's an errand she wants you to run."

Lydia did have a way of looking at a person as if she expected an apology for your being in good health when her son was not. As for Todd, he was making it a point not to look at Annabel at all. Theirs was not the storybook ending where shared danger welded a bond of fellowship between unfriendly parties. She supposed he blamed her for the abrupt end to his vacation.

Well, through the kitchen was the best route this morning, anyway. Annabel stopped in the back entry to ease a grocery bag from the rack where Aunt Lil stored them after shopping. For a wonder, it didn't rattle as Annabel tucked it under her arm.

In the garage, she selected a trowel from Uncle Axel's array of tools. A spade would be better for what she proposed to do, but she didn't see how she could handle that on a bike.

Ricky burst from the roadside brush to frisk around her as she wheeled onto the road. She didn't try to send

181

him back, partly because shouting at him might wake someone in the house, but more because she was glad of his company. What if she were wrong, and the ghost of Julia Craig hadn't been laid to rest with her mortal remains? What if it had been turned loose on the countryside instead?

Annabel kept an anxious eye on Ricky when she left the road and cut across the meadow to the old logging trail. He bounded along ahead of her on the trail, never once losing the crisp curl of his tail or showing the least hint of uneasiness.

The trail itself had been chopped and cleared into an almost respectable road to accommodate the vehicles that had passed over it to and from the cottage since the storm. No fear of missing it anymore. Wheel tracks led from it right up to the house.

Annabel rode around to the front.

There the door hung open and a little crooked, and the great killer pine lay in sawed lengths on the ground. She had to sit the bike a moment, clamping a lid on her memories while her palms grew damp.

Ricky nosed past her on a trail of his own that took him up to the door. He uttered an inquiring "Wuf?" in her direction and trotted on inside without hesitation, ears perked as high as their natural droop would allow.

Annabel felt the difference in the atmosphere as soon as she followed him over the doorsill. The house was empty. Quiet. But not silent, intently still. Just an ordinary quiet laced with small, ordinary sounds like the jay fluting his morning song nearby and the fly buzzing foolishly against a broken pane.

A path from door to stairs had been opened in the wreckage on the floor. At one side of it lay the old clock, face down. Its case was split open and a sifting of sawdust and plaster coated its jumbled works. It would not tick again.

All the same, Annabel didn't linger to marvel. Paper bag under her arm, she climbed quickly up the stairs. It had to be quickly or she couldn't bear to stand in that attic one more time, even knowing Julia Craig was gone.

The wardrobe was gone, too, moved to Uncle Axel's garage for safekeeping until her grandfather decided what was to be done with its contents. Nothing remained of Julia Craig's secret but the old lamp, sitting where it had been for forty-four years, and that decaying doll blanket bundled in a cardboard carton.

Annabel knelt by the carton and gingerly lifted an edge of the blanket. Traces of silver-gray hair, a few small bones—the answer that had come to her before dawn this morning. For what twisted reason no one now could know, Julia Craig had brought the body of Annie's cat, Macduff, up here to be stored in hiding with the other souvenirs.

Annabel slid the carton into her bag and carried it carefully down the stairs and out. Ricky, sneezing from his investigation of dusty corners in the front room, galloped to join her as she wheeled the bike back toward the big lilac behind the house.

The old tree stood broad and green as though there had never been any storm to speak of. This was where the little girl Annie and her cat had played together. This was where, in the picture Michael took, the blurred shape of a cat crouched, waiting. This was where Annabel dug a grave with the trowel and pressed the earth down over the neatly folded bag and what it held.

When she straightened finally, the feather of a breeze touched her face. The lilac leaves stirred softly with its passing and hung quiet.

She looked back one last time at the cottage. Was it an illusion, or had it sagged visibly in the past week? It looked shaky and exposed without its towering wall of pines, as if it would not stand against many more storms.

Ricky snuffed the trowel in Annabel's hand, then licked her knuckles as if to suggest there were more interesting things to do than stand meditating here. She scratched him under his chin, and swung onto the bike. How much easier life would be if people could give and take love as simply as animals did—no payment demanded in terms of gratitude, dependence, blighted dreams—if people could just learn to live and let live.

Her mood began to brighten as she left the logging road for the meadow. She had taken longer than she had expected on her errand. Breakfast was probably over, but she wouldn't get much flak on that account, particularly not from Uncle Axel. He credited her with having cleared the family name, and nothing she said or did these days could provoke his displeasure.

Besides, today was special. In a few hours her mother would be here. There was so much Annabel wanted to show her, so much to tell. Maybe her mother would find a second parting too hard and insist on Annabel going home with her. Maybe, too, she'd agree to inviting Donna down for a visit later in the summer.

"Wuf!" Ricky said warningly, coming to a standstill at the edge of the blacktop. A man and woman, who obviously thought the road was deserted, were strolling up ahead with their arms around each other.

"Quiet," Annabel told Ricky. "If people are happy, let them be."

She was easing back on her pedaling so as not to overtake the lovers too quickly when recognition struck. That woman was her mother. And the man—

The sweet promise of the day dissolved in a blaze of fury. She should have known. She should have known.

But, in fact, she had known. She'd only been pretending to herself that because her mother had failed to mention him, Donald Kimball might fail to intrude on their private lives this once.

Annabel shifted to top speed and bore down on them, jangling her bell as raucously as she could. The clinging arms swiftly unwound as she skidded to a stop a bike length beyond her mother.

"Annabel." Her mother was hugging her before Annabel's feet were both firmly on the ground.

There wasn't anything Annabel could do but hug back. There wasn't anything else she wanted to do. For that moment, everything was restored to how it should be. Donald was forgotten, left on the outside.

"How did you get here so soon?" Annabel asked. "Everybody said not to start looking for you until this afternoon."

"We left right after work and drove partway last night. As far as Appleton. Then we set out bright and early this morning."

That casual "we" jerked Annabel back to earth. And an overnight trip together. How cozy. She stiffened, glaring past her mother's shoulder to where Donald was petting Ricky, who, instead of bristling as he usually did at a stranger, was traitorously wagging his tail.

Donald grinned at her, his teeth a white flash of understanding beneath his moustache. "We stayed with my sister and her family. It was all very proper and aboveboard."

Her mother laughed. "Except that I think Donald either stole the present he brought you or strong-armed his sister into giving it up."

"I did her a favor," Donald said righteously. "She can never make up her mind which to give away and which to keep. She'd be overrun if the decisions were left totally to her."

Annabel stood watching them, taking note less of what they were saying than of the intimate, bantering tone they were using to say it. They sounded like a pair of teenagers in love. They even looked young, her mother especially—younger and fresher and softly aglow when she smiled at him.

Annabel twitched the lever of the bike bell as if by accident. "What are you talking about?"

"A kitten," her mother said. "It's in the car. Six weeks old and almost a perfect repeat of Muffin at that age, except for more white on the nose maybe. Donald's sister has the mother and a basket of kittens, but Donald spotted this one right away."

"Come on. I'll introduce you." Donald started walking again, looking ridiculously eager.

But why shouldn't he be eager? How could she accept a gift like this and not accept him, too, or at least begin to? And how could she refuse a tiny, warm, appealing kitten of her own again, to nurture and cuddle? She would be lost the minute she laid eyes on it, and Donald knew it. He was clever, all right. Calculating and clever.

"I've got to put this bike away first. And this trowel. I'll meet you at the house."

Without waiting for questions, she leaned over the handlebars and sped off, leaving him and her mother to follow as they would.

She cut across the lawn to avoid riding too close to Donald's blue-toned car parked on the drive. As long as she didn't see the kitten, she'd be all right. And if she did have to see it, definitely she would not touch it, not if she had to sit on her hands. Donald Kimball would learn she was not such a pushover to manipulate.

She went out the side door of the garage, around behind the house, and in through the kitchen, stalling for time. The kitchen was empty, the dishwasher chugging its testimony that she had indeed missed breakfast. As if she could choke down anything at this point, anyhow.

She washed her grubby hands at the sink and walked on toward the front of the house. Todd's mother was descending the stairs, a suitcase in her hand. No chance of anything intruding between her and her child.

"Ah, Annie. I know your parents are here, but if I could borrow you just a minute—"

Parents? Annabel opened her mouth, but she couldn't get her wind somehow.

"Mother," Todd shrilled from the living room, "I told you: the name is Annabel."

Astonishment carried Annabel alongside his mother to the living room door. "What did you say, Toddy?" Lydia asked.

Todd's fist was pounding a peevish rhythm against the padded arm of his chair. His leg in its cast rested on a footstool in front of him. "Annabel," he repeated, beating out the emphasis. "*Not* Annie."

His pale-fringed eyes encountered Annabel's, and the fist stopped an inch above the chair. Annabel, too, was suspended in mid-beat. She was remembering those same words flung at a beckoning image in a glass.

And so was Todd. The knowledge leaped like a spark between them. It was almost audible.

He swung his arm at her in a gesture more defensive than threatening. "Get out of here. What are you gawking at?"

He would never admit the truth, of course. But Annabel had no need to have it spoken. It was enough—it was everything—just to know she was not the only one who knew it.

"Now, Toddy," his mother reproved tolerantly. "She's going to scoot up and check the top shelves of your closet for us."

Annabel caught sight of herself in the mirror over the fireplace as she stepped back. Predictably, her hair was uncombed, but the new hair cut lent itself agreeably to a tousled look. She was wearing the plaid shirt and Donna's wide red belt she had laid out last night for her mother's arrival and in her haste this morning had put on first thing. The overall effect was attractively update and all-together. Curiously, the uncanny likeness to her grandmother was gone, reduced to a mere family resemblance.

Gone, too, was something scared that had long huddled within her, and with it something small and mean. She felt as tall inside as she was out, and the feeling was good.

"I'm sorry," she told Lydia, "but I can't just now. They're waiting for me outside."

And they were, her mother and Donald chatting by the car with Uncle Axel like vacationers without a care, but in fact waiting for a sign from her as to how to get on with their lives. As if she were a junior Julia Craig.

She had to wrestle only a little to make herself go down off the porch. Then she broke into a run and crossed the lawn in long, free strides, reaching out to her mother, and to Donald, and to the ball of gold-and-white fluff that began to purr as soon as she bent her cheek to it.

BEVERLY BUTLER, a native of Milwaukee, Wisconsin, began writing stories at fourteen, partly for typing practice so that she could rejoin her high school class after losing her sight. Her *Light a Single Candle*, which won the Clara Ingram Judson Award, and *Gift of Gold* are both based on her own experiences.

Her first novel, *Song of the Voyageur*, won Dodd, Mead's *Seventeenth Summer* Literary Competition, and her most recent story was *My Sister's Keeper*, winner of an Award of Merit from the State Historical Society of Wisconsin. Beverly Butler was graduated from Mount Mary College and holds an M.A. degree from Marquette University. She has received the Johnson Foundation Prize of the Council of Wisconsin Writers, and divides her time between writing and teaching creative writing courses.

She is married to Theodore V. Olsen, also a writer. They live in Rhinelander, Wisconsin.

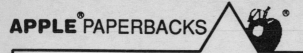